BLOOD PATHOGEN

A JOHN JORDAN MYSTERY THRILLER

MICHAEL LISTER

ISBN:

Ebook: 978-1-947606-60-9

Paperback: 978-1-947606-58-6

Hardback: 978-1-947606-59-3

Books by Michael Lister

(John Jordan Novels)
Power in the Blood
Blood of the Lamb
Flesh and Blood
(Special Introduction by Margaret Coel)
The Body and the Blood
Double Exposure
Blood Sacrifice
Rivers to Blood
Burnt Offerings
Innocent Blood
(Special Introduction by Michael Connelly)
Separation Anxiety
Blood Money
Blood Moon
Thunder Beach
Blood Cries
A Certain Retribution
Blood Oath
Blood Work
Cold Blood
Blood Betrayal
Blood Shot

Blood Ties
Blood Stone
Blood Trail
Bloodshed
Blue Blood
And the Sea Became Blood
The Blood-Dimmed Tide
Blood and Sand
A John Jordan Christmas
Blood Lure
Blood Pathogen

(Jimmy Riley Novels)
The Girl Who Said Goodbye
The Girl in the Grave
The Girl at the End of the Long Dark Night
The Girl Who Cried Blood Tears
The Girl Who Blew Up the World

(Merrick McKnight / Reggie Summers Novels)
Thunder Beach
A Certain Retribution
Blood Oath
Blood Shot

(Remington James Novels)
Double Exposure
(includes intro by Michael Connelly)
Separation Anxiety
Blood Shot

(Sam Michaels / Daniel Davis Novels)
Burnt Offerings
Blood Oath
Cold Blood
Blood Shot

(Love Stories)
Carrie's Gift

(Short Story Collections)
North Florida Noir
Florida Heat Wave
Delta Blues
Another Quiet Night in Desperation

(The Meaning Series)
Meaning Every Moment
The Meaning of Life in Movies

For Autumn,
Such a light! Such a gift!
I love and adore you!

THE JOHN JORDAN SERIES ON AUDIOBOOK

The entire John Jordan series is being produced on high quality audiobook. Start listening to these thrilling productions today. For more information and samples go to www. MichaelLister.com

BLOOD PATHOGEN

COVID-19

The virus that causes the COVID-19 disease emerged in Wuhan, China, in late 2019. Since then it has spread to some two hundred countries and territories and counting.

COVID-19 symptoms, which can range from mild to severe and may appear two to fourteen days after exposure to the virus, include but are not limited to cough, shortness of breath, fever, sore throat, loss of taste or smell, nausea, vomiting, and diarrhea.

As many as 80 percent of COVID-19 positive patients exhibit mild symptoms, and because most of the symptoms are non-specific and can mirror other more common illnesses like allergies or a cold, many COVID-19 carriers didn't realize they were spreading the virus, especially early in the outbreak.

As of February 23, fourteen COVID-19 cases had been diagnosed in the following six states: Arizona (one case), California (eight), Illinois (two), Massachusetts (one), Washington (one), and Wisconsin (one). Twelve of these fourteen cases were related to travel to China, and two cases occurred through person-to-person transmission to close household contacts of a person with confirmed COVID-19. An additional thirty-nine cases were reported among repatriated US citizens, residents, and their families returning from Hubei province, China (three) and from the Diamond Princess cruise ship that was docked in Yokohama, Japan (thirty-six). Thus, there have been fifty-three cases within the United States.

By early March, the number of global cases continued to rise, nearing the hundred thousand mark, with a death toll of over three thousand.

A few days earlier, the Trump administration issued its highest-level warning, known as a "do not travel" warning, for areas in Italy and South Korea that are most affected by the virus.

US officials approved widespread testing.

The Centers for Disease Control and Prevention at the US Department of Health and Human Services lifted all federal restrictions on testing for the coronavirus after the CDC's first attempt to produce a diagnostic test kit failed.

From the CDC headquarters in Atlanta, President Trump said, "Anybody that wants a test can get a test. The tests are all perfect, like the letter was perfect, the transcription was perfect, right?"

COVID-19

"COVID-19 turned out to be my worst nightmare come to life," Dr. Anthony Fauci, the White House health advisor said in a recent interview with the BIO Digital virtual health care conference. "It's something that's highly transmissible . . . In a period—if you just think about it—in a period of four months, it has devastated the world."

Dr. Fauci is the director of the National Institute of Allergy and Infectious Diseases, and the most trusted voice of the COVID-19 crisis in the United States.

"That's millions and millions of infections worldwide," he went on to say. "And it isn't over yet. And it's condensed in a very, very small time frame."

FRIDAY, MARCH 6, 2020

Friday, March 6, 2020
402 confirmed cases and 14 deaths in the US

1

———

"Should we cancel?" Jules asks. "How bad is this coronavirus thing going to get?"

It's a good question—one we don't have a good answer for. Mixed messages and lack of information and guidance means we don't have much to go on. Only twelve hundred cases in a country of three hundred and fifty million people isn't many, but seeing how rapidly and prolifically it has spread and devastated other countries certainly seems a portent worth heeding.

It's early March 2020. Dad, his wife Verna, his older sister Julia, and I are standing behind Dad and Verna's farmhouse watching the rental company erect the enormous clear-plastic event tent not unlike the one they set up in the exact same spot last year for Merrill and Zaire's wedding.

The farmhouse is about seventy yards from a secluded and serene lake and the tent fits perfectly parallel between the two, creating a celebratory atmosphere delicately lit by a thousand looping string lights and allowing for the beauty of the cypress-tree-rimmed lake and the surrounding flat fields while keeping out mosquitos, bugs, wind, and rain.

"As you can imagine," Jules says, "Nell thinks we should cancel it and Lavinia thinks it's our patriotic duty to do it."

Jules Jordan, Lavinia Pritchett, and Nellie Bell Harbuck, known collectively as the Tupelo Queens, are the best of friends and have been for over six decades, going all the way back to their days in grammar school together.

Though strikingly different and often at odds socially, financially, politically, philosophically, and religiously, the three women have a shared interest in the arts, especially music and theater, and that most powerful of connective tissue, a shared history, including each being crowned Tupelo Queen at various times at Wewa's annual Tupelo Festival back in their day.

"It's so gracious of y'all to allow us to throw our little soirée here," Jules says.

With no apparent animosity, Dad and Aunt Jules have never been particularly close. Perhaps it's their gender and age difference—she's seven years his senior—or maybe it's unspoken and unresolved childhood trauma, but it came as a surprise to all of us when she asked her little brother if she could have her seventy-fourth birthday party at his farm.

Like so many aging entertainers who attempt to maintain a stage and camera readiness, Jules doesn't look like a woman in her seventies. Although she has certain signs of aging—some of the thickening and heaviness that time and a changing metabolism can cause to cling to us. As she often says, she is "spread out like a cold supper" and as she continues to age it's her right and responsibility to take up ever more room in the world. Still, she has an allure and attractiveness emanating out of her and the sheer magnetism and power of a performer's personality.

"And we're happier than a pig in shit to be doing it here," she continues, "and though we gals are known for being a touch theatrical, we have zero interest in staging a real-life production of Poe's *Masque of the Red Death* in your beautiful backyard."

Among the many things they're known for—being the most colorful and popular standards trio in the region and staging the most popular community theater plays—the Tupelo Queens are perhaps most well known for their parties, which not only include traditional holiday extravaganzas but also the birthday bashes they each throw for themselves and at which they each attempt to outdo the others.

No one in the US is canceling events or large gatherings yet, but every indication is that's the best and most proficient way to slow down the spread of the virus, and there are health experts saying that's what we need to do to flatten the curve of infections of the highly contagious, newly named COVID-19.

"I realize they're busier than a moth in a mitten putting up that big ol' plastic bubble, but I just want y'all to know that I won't pitch a hissy fit if y'all think we need to close the curtain on this little production."

Like so many of the more colorful people in our neck of the woods, Jules's speech is seasoned with Southern expressions and idioms, and like her two Tupelo Queens buddies, also often with theatrical and musical expressions.

Verna says, "I just don't know enough about it. Do you really think it's here—in our little town?"

That is the *to be or not to be* question about a highly infectious virus for which the vast majority of carriers are asymptomatic.

"It's your call," Dad says. "We're just providing a little patch of grass. Up to you what you do with it. Why not let them finish putting up the tent, talk to the others, do a little research, and make your final decision a little closer to the time. You've got more'n a week to decide."

She nods. "Thank you, Jack. Always give wise, sound counsel. I appreciate that. So glad you're sheriff again. That's what I'll do. I look forward to this all year, but I'd feel plum terrible if someone got sick just trying to celebrate another one of my many trips around the sun."

2

———

Dad is the sheriff of Potter County again.

Planning to run again this year, he was appointed by the governor to finish out the term when Hugh Glenn, the deputy who had beaten him in the last election, suddenly and mysteriously stepped down for personal reasons.

What seems to be a majority of Potter County citizens are pleased to have him back in the position, but there's no way he'll run unopposed this fall, and no guarantees he'll win. And though for now his health is holding up, there's also no guarantee it will.

The two of us are in his black sheriff's SUV headed toward the small African Methodist Episcopal church out on Highway 73.

We are going to meet with the Reverend Willie Baker, the minister of the fledgling church.

Dad asked me along because I had worked with Willie when I was a chaplain at Gulf Correctional Institution and he was an inmate.

I had been a prison chaplain for many years after returning to Florida from Atlanta—continuing to do it part-time when I became an investigator with the Gulf County Sheriff's Department—and had only pulled the pin and retired from it when Hurricane Michael hit the region and decimated the prison.

I love being an investigator, but I miss being a chaplain, and look for opportunities to teach and speak and counsel when I can.

The small, white, cinder block building of the AME church is at the end of a short dirt road in a hardwood hammock that provides a hedge from the highway and a canopy from the sun.

In disrepair and in need of a fresh coat of paint and surrounded by thick woods, the church appears abandoned, which in a way it is—by all but a few ardent faithful whose families had attended the gathering of the saints here for generations.

As we pull up and step out of the vehicle, Willie appears in front of the church, standing in front of the old wooden double doors as if guarding them.

"Mr. Baker," Dad says, extending his hand as we walk over to him.

"Reverend," he corrects as he shakes Dad's hand.

"Sorry," Dad says. "Reverend. I'm Jack Jordan and I think you know my son, John."

He nods toward me. "Chaplain," he says. "Good to see you. Thought I'd've seen you before now. Had hoped you'd attend service, come hear me preach."

"Sorry, I haven't yet," I say, "but I will. Soon as I can."

"I'll hold you to it," he says. "So what brings the sheriff out to my humble little church?"

"As you know, we have a very progressive mayor," Dad says.

In its most recent and historical election, Pottersville had elected its first African American mayor, a doctor who had grown up here and had returned a few years back to care for his aging parents.

Willie nods.

"Well, he's a doctor and evidently has many good friends who are virologists, and as I'm sure you also know, he's announced that he's considering implementing a shelter-in-place order or at least an order against large gatherings for Pottersville, because he's convinced that's the only way to slow the spread of the COVID-19 virus."

Willie nods again.

"If he does, it'll be my job to enforce it," Dad continues. "And if it comes to that I want to be able to do that as smoothly and with as little friction as possible."

"I'm sure you do," Willie says.

"It's come to my attention that you said from the pulpit Sunday that if the order is given, you plan to disobey it and expect your congregation to do the same."

"You got hidden cameras in my sanctuary?" Willie asks. "Find it hard to believe a member of my congregation would rat me out like that."

"No one ratted you out," Dad says, seeming uncomfortable even repeating such words back to him. "It's a small town. News travels fast. Gossip faster. It was probably as innocent as one of your parishioners innocently mentioning it to a family member or friend and it spreading from there. But all of that is beside the point. What I need to know is if it's true."

Willie nods again. "It is."

"You plan to disobey a direct order from the mayor given to protect the lives of your congregation?"

"If that order says we can't gather in the house of God to honor and worship the Lord."

"You realize it would only be for a few Sundays," Dad says, "and it would be to save lives?"

"I do."

"You could conduct your service online from your home," I say.

"Most of my congregation are elderly and not online, and

when God through his word told us not to forsake the assembling of ourselves together, he didn't say until it wasn't convenient or dangerous."

Like so many damaged people, Willie had become radicalized—something his brand of jailhouse religion certainly contributed to.

"Well," Dad says, "I hope you'll seriously reconsider . . . because if the order is given, I'll have to enforce it. It would only be for a few short weeks and it would be primarily to protect elderly people like those in your congregation."

"I'm willing to be a martyr," he says. "I'm not willing to compromise my convictions."

"Martyr?" Dad says. "Nobody said anything about becoming a martyr. The most that would happen is that you'd be sent home."

"And if I refuse to go?"

"Then you'd be arrested, not martyred."

"Yeah, 'cause that's what happens to innocent black men in America."

I don't agree with what he says he's going to do or most of his rhetoric, but it is hard to argue this last point.

He turns to me. "What would you do, Chaplain?"

"Comply with the mayor's very reasonable order."

"Then you're not the man I thought you were."

"Happy to disappoint you," I say.

3

"Well, I hope that uppity . . . mayor don't do nothin' like that," Leviticus Lanier is saying.

He's a white Holiness Pentecostal preacher with a small congregation on Second Street. Like Willie Baker, he's uneducated and untrained, has a troubled past, and approaches religion through a literal-minded fire and brimstone lens. Unlike Baker, his religion is infused with a harshness and underlying racism.

"But if he does . . ." he continues, "no, we won't be *complyin'*."

"You'd put your congregation at risk of infection or arrest over a couple of weeks of having to do your services online?" Dad asks.

"God's not gonna let us get infected in his holy sanctuary," he says. "And it won't be the first time God's people have been persecuted. We expect it."

"I'm here as a courtesy because of what you've been posting online about disobeying the temporary order not to gather if it comes," Dad says. "I'm trying to prevent any issues before they arise. You can hardly call that persecution."

"If you jail us for worshiping God, I don't know what else to call it."

"If Mayor Long gives the order, it will be to protect our citizens from the spread of a deadly virus and it will be temporary. And it will be enforced."

"We obey the laws of God, not the laws of man," he says. "No matter what."

"Please reconsider putting your congregation through anything like this if it comes to it. I don't want to arrest you or anyone else—and the elderly and infirmed members don't need to be in close contact with people in the jail any more than they do people in the church. For their sake please think about that."

"'He was wounded for our transgressions,'" Lanier says, quoting the passage from Isaiah. "'He was bruised for our iniquities. The chastisement for our peace was upon Him. And by His stripes we are healed.'"

Dad looks at me.

"He's saying God won't let them get sick," I explain, "that Jesus took their sickness and became their healing."

Dad looks back at Lanier, who nods.

"And Sheriff, be best for you to remember this—" he says. "'No weapon formed against us will prosper.' You'll be heaping a world of trouble on your head if you mess with me. For the Lord sayeth, 'Touch not mine anointed and do my prophets no harm.' You've been warned."

"No, sir," Dad says, "*you* have."

4

———

H *ELP!*

The single-word text from Jasmine Carter comes as I'm leaving Dad's farm and about to head home, and causes me to turn a different direction when I pull out of the long pasture fence-lined drive.

Following Hurricane Michael's decimation of the area and a couple of cases related to it, and two cold cases—the Magdalene Dacosta case over in Sandcastle and the Naomi Newman and Sasha Grande case in the river swamps not far from Pottersville—it had been a relatively quiet year.

Most of the cases I worked were more typical and it was obvious nearly from the beginning who the culprits were, so I had less stress and demands on me and far more free time. I had spent the vast majority of that extra time with my family and friends, in particular Anna, Johanna, Taylor, Carla and John Paul, Dad and Verna, Merrill and Zaire, Jake, Nancy, Reggie and Merrick, and Sam and Daniel. I had also spent some of that time with my own cold case files—specifically certain aspects of the Atlanta Child Murders—and some ministerial work, which consisted mostly of pastoral and spiritual growth counseling, much if it online. But perhaps the most rewarding and fulfilling and at times frustrating work I had done was with Nash Carter, a fourteen-year-old troubled teen whose mom Jasmine was increasingly neglectful and whose dad had mostly been MIA since he was born.

Pulling into their concrete driveway, I find them in the front yard—Nash, Jasmine, Jasmine's boyfriend Paul Branch, and Jasmine and Paul's five-year-old son Harley.

Paul has Nash pinned against the only tree in the yard, a large live oak with long, spreading branches.

Pressing him against the white-gray bark with his left forearm, Paul is pointing at Nash with his right hand, yelling at him, as Jasmine, balancing Harley on her hip, pleads with Paul to let him go.

I jump out of my truck and rush over to them.

"Let him go, Paul," I say as I come up on them. "Now."

Paul turns to me, all red-faced, narrow-eyed, snarling-mouthed. "Stay the fuck out of this, John. Got nothing to do with you. I ain't gonna hit him, but he's gonna learn some fuckin' manners and show me some goddamn respect."

Tears stream from Nash's eyes and he's heaving trying to catch his breath.

"Last chance to let him go on your own," I say.

"Oh, you're a tough guy now?" he says, turning toward me. "That it? Mr. Peace and Love Preacher Compassionate Cop is a badass now?"

In turning toward me he lets go of Nash, which I think is his way of doing it without appearing to consciously do what I told him to.

He's shorter than me, but at least ten years younger and far more muscular, and could probably kick my ass in a street fight.

He takes a step toward me as Nash rushes to his mother behind him.

Without moving forward or backward, I shift my weight and prepare to defend myself if he attacks.

Stopping a few feet from me, he glances down at the gun and badge on my belt.

"Out of your jurisdiction over here," he says. "If you didn't have that little pop gun on your belt and if your daddy wasn't the fake sheriff here, I'd teach you some manners along with that little bastard."

"*Paul*, stop it," Jasmine says. "The only one lacking manners right now is you."

He turns toward her in surprise instead of anger. "You really think I'm in the wrong here?" he asks, his anger quickly dissipating, his countenance softening.

I step between them.

His transformation is so sudden it's startling—and suspicious.

"You need to move," he says, his anger spiking again. "I've never hit a woman or a kid and I never will, but I'll beat the shit out of you if you try to come between me and my family."

"*Paul*," Jasmine says again. "Stop it. You're being ridiculous. Nash was a little disrespectful but you overreacted and John's just trying to help."

That stops him.

For a long moment, he stands seeming to consider what she has said, calming down, gathering himself, and though I find this transformation as suspicious as the previous one, it at least lasts longer and can be seen taking place.

Being around someone as seemingly shallow and insincere and double-minded as Paul creates emotional whiplash in those around him, and not for the first time I wish I could take Nash away from the chaos.

"He shows nothin' but disrespect for me," he says to her around me. "It was just the last straw, you know? Sorry I overreacted. I am. It just built up, you know? And I don't want anyone ever actin' like they have to defend my family from me."

"Well, you're acting like somebody needs to," she says.

"Sorry. I just lost my temper."

He's so quick to apologize that I question its sincerity, but like his nearly instant transformation from rage to reasonableness, it seems genuine.

"It's Nash you need to apologize to," she says.

He nods slowly and frowns. "Sorry, man. I really am. I . . . I got carried away. I shouldn't'a acted like that and said those things. My bad."

Nash doesn't respond.

"And John, I know you're just tryin' to help. Sorry for the shit I said to you too."

I nod, but give no indication I'm buying what he's now peddling.

"If you ever lay a finger on Nash again—or any of us," Jasmine says, "we're through. Understand?"

Paul drops his head and nods but doesn't say anything.

"And I think you need to go," she adds. "Stay at your place tonight. I'll talk with Nash and see what he's comfortable with and then the three of us can talk in a day or so."

"Really?" Paul says. "I have to go? We can't talk about it now? I said I was sorry. I didn't mean anything bad by it . . . I was just holding him there, makin' him listen to me. I didn't hurt him. I wouldn't. I've never hurt anyone. I've never hit anyone—I mean, never a woman or a child."

"I know," she says. "And you know I wouldn't be with you if you had, but we all just need some time to settle down and think things through and regroup."

"Okay," Paul says, blinking back tears, "but y'all are my family. I don't want to lose y'all. Don't throw away all we have over one moment of bad temper. Please."

5

———

"Anything like that ever happen before?" I ask.

Nash shakes his head.

The two of us are in my truck, headed toward Wewa and home.

After Paul left, Jasmine, Nash, and I had talked for a while, during which she asked if I could spend even more time with Nash and I had suggested that he stay with us tonight.

"Never?" I ask. "Nothin' even close?"

He shakes his head again. "They haven't been back together long."

Paul and Jasmine break up and get back together so often their relationship is more like that of wounded adolescents instead of actual adults.

"I'm so sorry that happened to you," I say. "I know how scary it must have been. Paul's a big guy, got muscles on his muscles."

"You weren't scared," he says.

"Sure I was," I say. "And I'm a grown man. If that had happened when I was fourteen, before I was fully developed and had a little experience dealing with bullies . . . I'd've wet myself. You did great. I just want you to know it's okay to be scared and to feel frustrated when someone overpowers you like that."

"I want to . . ."

"To what? It's okay. Tell me."

"I want to . . . beat him with my bare fists to a bloody pulp."

I nod. "Of course you do," I say. "What he did to you, how he made you feel—helpless and afraid. Think how Harley would feel if you did something like that to him, how unfair it would be if you did. He'd feel the same way. And you'd be just as wrong as Paul was if you did. What you're feeling is normal —a natural reaction to being bullied by a bigger, stronger man. Can't help what we feel. Only what we do with it. You can see it for what it is, process what you're feeling and let it out in productive ways, or you can let it eat you up inside and turn you into a scared, angry, hate-filled person who punishes himself and others—bullying those smaller and weaker than you. You get to decide what kind of man you're going to be. Just like I did and do, and Paul and Merrill and your dad and my dad did."

"I know I don't want to be like them," he says.

"Who?"

"Paul and my parents. Why is everybody so fuckin' fake?"

"Figuring out who you are, the kind of person you want to be and actually becoming it, being true to yourself no matter the circumstance or situation is a lot harder than you would think."

"Must be. 'Cause people sure as shit don't do it, do they? My mom was this big hippie chick—all natural everything, envi- ronmentalist, herbalist, grew her own food, homeschooled us, didn't believe in technology, doctors, Western medicine, recy- cled everything, leave-no-footprint kind of shit, and then Paul comes along and just like that . . . all that stuff's not so impor- tant anymore. Not sayin' she stopped it all—she still makes me and Harley live that way—but now she sees doctors and she's started taking prescription pills, something everybody knows but Grandma Nell . . . and now she's all *Paul says this* and *Paul thinks that.*"

"How's he treat her and you and Harley?"

"Treats her like a queen most of the time. They're usually all . . . up on each other and lovey-dovey, not like today. He treats me okay—nothing like Harley, but okay—'specially with . . . how I am to him."

"How is that?"

"Like a creatine-taking, steroid-popping, mirror-gazing, swole dumbbell should be."

"You're a lot smarter than Paul, aren't you?"

"Who isn't?"

"I understand why you resent him and don't want him with your mom or in your life," I say. "I really do, but . . . if we mock, make fun of, or belittle someone who's not as smart as us, then we're bullying them with our brains instead of our muscles— but it's still bullying."

6

───────

"Mommy," Taylor says in a loud whisper, "Nash is on his phone."

We are all seated at our kitchen table, preparing to eat together—me, Anna, Taylor, Johanna, and Nash—and as he has been for the entire time he's been here, Nash is fiddling with his phone.

Anna smiles and looks at Nash as he's looking up from his device. "House rule," Anna says. "No phones at the dinner table. Besides, you're far too handsome for us just to see the top of your head."

"Sorry," he says, quickly slipping his phone into his pocket.

"It's no problem," I say. "You didn't know. We just do it so we focus on interacting with each other."

He nods. "I get it. It's a good rule."

"Who wants to say the blessing?" Anna asks.

"I do, I do," Taylor says, raising her hand.

"Okay. Thank you."

"Lord," Taylor says, bowing her head and closing her eyes before anyone else has had a chance to, "thank you for the beautiful day and the great food. Thank you for Mommy and

Daddy and Johanna and our special guest, Nash. And be with all the sick people. Amen."

"Hope you're hungry, Nash," Anna says. "I made a ton."

"Yes, ma'am. Looks good."

Anna has made spaghetti and meatballs, garlic knots, green beans, tossed salad, and has a key lime pie waiting in the wings, out of sight on the counter next to the refrigerator.

After fixing our plates, we haven't been eating long when Taylor says, "Let's do High Low, Mommy."

"Okay," Anna says. "Nash, you remember High Low? Everyone tells the high and low points of their day."

He nods.

"I'll go first," she says. "High was getting to make this meal for y'all and getting to enjoy it with you. Low was when a prosecutor in a case I'm working on was rude and condescending to me on a conference call, which made it difficult to address. Left me angry and frustrated."

"I'm very sorry that happened," I say. "Clearly he's an insecure and ignorant . . . ah behind, and I'm sorry he made you feel frustrated or anything other than amazing."

"It's long since over now," she says. "I get to spend my evening with you fine examples of humanity and that makes my high a lot, lot higher than my low."

I glance at Nash to see how he's processing what Anna is saying but am unable to read him.

Taylor says, "My turn. My turn."

"High low," I say.

"Mommy put me in time-out this afternoon," she says.

"Is that your high or low?" I ask.

"Low, silly," she says.

"Good, 'cause if that was your high, it was a rough day. What's your high?"

"I got invited to Madison Little's birthday party," she says. "And it's a sleepover in her grandma's cabin."

"Cool," I say. "That sounds amazing."

"We've already talked about it," Anna says, "and she knows it might get postponed because of the coronavirus."

"I sure hope not," Taylor says.

"Okay," Anna says, "who's next? Nash, Johanna, or John?"

Johanna has been particularly quiet tonight, and I wonder if it's Nash's presence or something else.

"Johanna?" I ask.

"I'm still thinking. Y'all go ahead."

"Me too," Nash says when I shift my gaze over to him. "You go ahead."

"Well, like Anna, my high is being here with you all tonight. It's so cool to have Nash with us and I wish it happened more often."

"Me too," Taylor says.

"Me three," Anna says.

"My low was seeing someone I care about being treated very badly by a bully," I say. "It hurt my heart and made me think of how unfair it was and how often it had happened to me and how it made me feel when it did."

"Did you arrest him, Daddy?" Taylor asks.

"Shoulda shot him," Nash says.

"Can't shoot people when they don't act like they should," I say, "'cause that's all of us from time to time."

"Like I was in time-out today," Taylor says.

"Exactly," Anna says.

"It's not the same," he says. "Some people need to be put down like dogs."

TUESDAY, MARCH 10, 2020

Tuesday, March 10, 2020
1,300 confirmed cases and 31 deaths in the US

"For a while, life is not going to be how it used to be in the United States," Dr. Anthony Fauci says on CNN's *State of the Union* Sunday. "We have to just accept that if we want to do what's best for the American public. The outbreak in the US could get as bad as Italy if the public does not take action to prevent the spread of the virus. I think we should be overly aggressive and get criticized for overreacting. I think Americans should be prepared that they are going to have to hunker down significantly more than we as a country are doing."

"Well, this was unexpected," President Trump says on Capitol Hill after meeting with Republican senators. "This was something that came out of China, and it hit us and many other countries. You look at the numbers, I see the numbers with just by watching you folks. I see it—it's over one hundred different countries. And it hit the world. And we're prepared, and we're doing a great job with it. And it will go away. Just stay calm. It will go away."

So last year 37,000 Americans died from the common flu. It averages between 27,000 and 70,000 per year. Nothing is shut down, life & the economy go on. At this moment there are 546 confirmed cases of CoronaVirus, with 22 deaths. Think about that!

March 9 tweet from President Trump

7

______

"We're just seeking a little guidance, dear," Jules is saying. "We're about as lost on all this as last year's Easter eggs."

She's wearing a vintage blue maxi dress with embroidered patterns of sunbaked reds, greens, and golds, which accentuates her dark skin tone and thick black hair

The Tupelo Queens had asked if I'd see if Zaire Monroe, Merrill's wife and an MD, would be willing to talk to them about the coronavirus, and Merrill had said as long as I was present since he was coming too, so Anna and I were hosting the little get together.

We are all in our living room—me and Anna, Merrill and Zaire, and the three Tupelo Queens—Jules Jordan, Lavinia Pritchett, and Nellie Bell Harbuck.

Like Jules, Lavinia and Nellie carry themselves like entertainers. They are spry and energetic and attractive—particularly for women in their seventies—and seem to expect others to notice and pay attention to them. They've maintained their figures, dress stylishly, and are never seen without their hair fixed and their makeup on.

"It's just that we keep hearing conflicting reports," Nellie says. "Got us as confused as a fart in a fan factory."

Dressed like an aging flower child, Nellie appears to have just come from a love-in or sit-in or music festival, and though her floral pattern front-knot dress makes it hard to imagine where she has it hidden, no one would question the fact that she has pot on her at all times.

"This past year's been mighty hard on us," Jules says. "We're hangin' on like a hair on a biscuit, but it ain't been easy."

Following the hurricane, which had affected them all in varying degrees, Jules had lost her husband to heart disease, Lavinia had lost her first great-grandchild to the whooping cough, and Nellie Bell's fifth husband had informed her he was gay and divorced her.

"We look forward to our birthday bashes all year long every year, but in a year like this one when we all need a little hope and happiness, we—well, you can imagine."

Though the Tupelo Queens are known for their epic Halloween costume monster mashup, a Fourth of July firework show and street dance, a *Same Old Lang Syne* New Year's Eve formal, and a winter wonderland Christmas ball, the highlight of their social party-throwing calendar is their successive birthday bashes, which fall in March, April, and May, beginning with Jules's and ending with Lavinia's.

"But as much as we're hankerin' to have our hootenannies," Nellie says, "we wouldn't want the Tupelo Queens to be known as the Typhoid Marys after our shindigs killed off our friends."

Lavinia says to Zaire, "Tell them they're overreacting and have got their panties in a wad over a hoax."

Dressed the most conservatively of the Queens, Lavinia's gray and pink summer-casual V-neck long sleeve maxi dress shows off a figure most twenty-year-olds would be proud of.

"It's no hoax," Zaire says. "And it's no joke. It's spreading across the globe and it will get far worse here in the States before it gets better. It's not being taken seriously enough and too little too late is being done about it."

Lavinia rolls her eyes.

"I've been monitoring the outbreak and spread closely," Zaire continues, "and based on what it has done in other countries and based on our response so far, I expect the disease to not just impact the US but to devastate it."

Lavinia shakes her head. "No, the president said it's all under control. We only have a few cases and we'll have zero soon. People like you are overreacting."

"People like *me*?" Zaire says.

"I just meant . . . anyone sayin' what you're sayin'. The president's political enemies and the media are blowing this all out of proportion."

According to Jules, Lavinia had never been this obtuse, conspiratorial, or blindly partisan before, and had only become so under the influence of her most recent husband Max—a conspiracy theorist and online activist with anti-social tendencies who has limited her daily intake of information to that which confirms the bias of a single worldview.

"That's objectively, verifiably not true," Zaire says, her voice calm and kind, but firm. "You asked for my opinion as a doctor and I'm giving it to you. And what I'm sharing with you is not partisan."

"I look forward to the day when everything isn't so cotton pickin' politicized," Jules says. "But I'm not sure I'll live long enough to see it."

"It's not based on media reports," Zaire continues. "It's not based on what any politician or people with political agendas are saying. It comes from reading the medical reports, from hearing what experts in the field around the world are saying."

Merrill says, "Every single day we are confronted with shit we don't want to hear, shit we wish wasn't true. We can ignore it, deny it, or allow it to change our perceptions and calculations. You asked for an educated opinion and that's what my brilliant, beautiful wife is giving you. You don't have to like it. You don't have to act on it. But you do have to show her the respect she deserves."

"Wasn't meaning any disrespect, dear," Lavinia says. "Just telling you what I've heard and read."

He smiles. "What we hear and read is only as good as the source it comes from and the agenda of the person saying or writing it."

Lavinia looks from Jules back to Zaire. "How many people died of the flu last year?"

"This isn't the flu," Nellie Bell says. "No matter what you've heard."

"Nellie Bell, don't you go gettin' uppity with me," Lavinia says. "Someone who doesn't believe in Western medicine and thinks home remedies, crystals, and rubbing your bare feet on *Mother Earth* can cure everything best not be lecturing me about anything—especially the flu."

Zaire says, "I don't know exactly, and it fluctuates from year to year, but I'd say the 2018–2019 flu season killed between thirty-four and thirty-eight thousand people in the US."

"What does that have to do with anything?" Jules asks.

"Y'all are panicking over the flu," Lavinia says.

"We're not *panicking* over anything."

"There's still so much we don't know," Zaire says, "which is part of the problem, but every indication is that COVID-19 is more infectious, spreads more easily and quickly, and is more deadly than the flu. Plus we have no vaccine for COVID-19."

"Doesn't matter 'cause she wouldn't take it anyway," Lavinia says.

"Let's talk specifically about this weekend," Jules says. "Should we not have our event? I understand what you're saying about the coronavirus coming to the US and what it will do, but is it here already? Will we be putting people at risk by getting together?"

"It is here," Zaire says. "In the US. We have confirmed cases and deaths and they're on the rise. Has it come to our little part of the world? We don't know for sure. And we won't until we are able to do adequate testing. It's possible, even likely, that rural areas like ours won't be as affected as larger metropolitan areas with far more international travel, but . . . and this is the thing to remember . . . it only takes one carrier, many of whom are asymptomatic, for it to spread—especially if a large group of people are in close proximity of the carrier for an extended period of time."

"So you're saying cancel Jules's birthday," Lavinia says.

"That's not what she said," Nellie Bell says. "Nobody's birthday is being canceled."

"I meant the party and you know it."

"Is that what you're sayin'?" Jules asks. "I'm asking for your recommendation of what we should do."

Zaire takes in a deep breath and lets it out in a long, slow sigh. "On one end of the spectrum is the abundance of caution and canceling the event. On the other is a reckless disregard for reality that says carry on as if there is no highly infectious and deadly virus going around. And somewhere in the middle is having a smaller gathering while taking steps to mitigate the potential for infection."

Jules turns and looks at Lavinia and Nellie. "All hearts and minds clear?"

They both nod noncommittally.

"Speak up," Jules says. "Anything else for the good of the order?"

They both look like they have something to say, but both shake their heads and remain silent.

"Thank you," Jules says to Zaire. "You've been so helpful to us, and I can't tell you how much we appreciate it. Least now we might be able to figure out whether to check our ass or scratch our watch."

Nellie Bell says, "I did think of something else I want to ask. Doctor Monroe, would you mind telling us what you'd do?"

"Not at all," Zaire says. "If it were my birthday, I'd either cancel it or make it a small affair with my few closest friends and family members. If it were Merrill's I'd still have it—just on a much smaller scale and implement as many precautions as possible."

Jules nods and smiles. "If we do decide to do a scaled-back version with precautions, could you give us a list of what those precautions might be?"

"Of course."

"And this is something we all need to pay attention to, girls," Jules says. "This isn't just going to affect my birthday. Sounds like this could get far worse by next month on your birthday, Nellie Bell, and even worse the month after that on yours, Lavinia."

WEDNESDAY, MARCH 11, 2020

Wednesday, March 11, 2020
1,700 confirmed cases and 37 deaths in the US

"To keep new cases from entering our shores, we will be suspending all travel from Europe to the United States for the next thirty days. The new rules will go into effect Friday at midnight. These restrictions will be adjusted subject to conditions on the ground," President Trump says in a televised Oval Office address to the nation.

FRIDAY, MARCH 13, 2020

Friday, March 13, 2020
2,700 confirmed cases and 49 deaths in the US

President Trump, who declares a national emergency, makes millions of dollars in funds available to states.

"We have forty people right now," President Trump says at a Rose Garden press conference. "Forty. Compare that with other countries that have many, many times that amount. And one of the reasons we have forty and others have—and, again, that number is going up, just so you understand. And a number of cases, which are very small, relatively speaking—it's going up. But we've done a great job because we acted quickly. We acted early. And there's nothing we could have done that was better than closing our borders to highly infected areas."

8
———

Though the rented tent still stands in Dad's backyard, on Saturday Jules's birthday takes place in her riverfront tidewater cottage several miles away.

Far more common in the Carolinas than here, Jules took the raised Southern tidewater cottage design and made it her own, adding a wide wraparound porch, a backdoor boardwalk down to a dock on the Apalachicola River, and a small, fully functioning theater with a red velour curtained stage and state-of-the-art lighting and sound design.

Following Zaire's recommendations, Jules has limited the attendees, is receiving her guests in staggered shifts, and has asked that everyone maintain a safe distance from each other and refrain from kissing, hugging, and even shaking hands. Never more than ten people in a room at a time and attempt to remain at least six feet apart. Birthday cake on the back porch, presents in the parlor, wait staff to a minimum—and them serving as enforcers and bouncers as much as anything else.

The Tupelo Queens and their families are, or course, permitted to be present the entire evening, but everyone else is allotted twenty minutes to drop off their gift, grab a piece of cake, and wish the birthday girl many happy returns.

Entertainment to be provided by said Tupelo Queens and to include arguing and bickering over religion, politics, and culture, musical selections from the Andrews to the Pointer Sisters, and comedic scenes from favorite plays—regardless of whether the playwright intended for the scene to be comedic or not.

The first person Anna and I run into is Carla Pearson, our unrelated grown stepdaughter and the mother of John Paul, the closest thing to a son we have.

Like the other servers, she's wearing black slacks, a white shirt, and a black bowtie, and carries a silver tray of refreshments.

We're surprised to see her. She usually asks us to keep John Paul when she works.

"This is a great gig," she says. "So much fun and crazy good money. Couldn't pass it up."

"Who has John Paul?"

"I knew you two would be here," she says. "So I got Lacy to do it. She needs the money anyway, and she's watching him at my place so she can put him down and I can just slip in when I'm done here."

She's overselling the situation because she knows we have reservations about Lacy, a lost twenty-something with a history of bad boyfriends and even worse choices, who lives in the same low-income apartment complex as Carla and John Paul.

"If it'll make y'all feel better, go by and check on them on your way home," she says. "I've got to get back to work."

She turns and takes a few steps, then turns back and extends the silver tray. "Beverage?"

"Sure," Anna says. "Thanks."

"I've got Chardonnay and Merlot," she says.

"Chardonnay for me, please," Anna says.

"Merlot for me," I say. "Thank you."

She shakes her head and twists her lips a bit. "I'll never get used to you drinking."

"It's mostly just a prop," I say. "The little bit I drink will be medicinal."

When Carla is gone we step into the parlor and place Jules's gift on the table in front of her.

She's speaking with Tom and Randall Foster, her recently deceased husband's two sons.

She breaks off mid-sentence to say, "Thank you two so much for coming. I'm thrilled you're here."

Her conversation with Tom and Randall seems civil enough —which is surprising, given that they've accused her of stealing their inheritance and are suing her to get it back.

"I said no gifts."

"But we knew you didn't mean it," I say.

"That's true," she says. "I'd've been butt-hurt for weeks if people would've showed up without presents."

"Sorry to have interrupted," I say. "We're gonna go mingle. We'll see you in a little while."

"Don't miss the champagne toast and performance," she says. "It'll be in the theater at 9:00 and it's going to be a hoot."

"Wouldn't miss it," Anna says.

Crossing the foyer, we make the mistake of entering the den, where Nellie and Lavinia are holding forth religion and politics and anything else they can come up with to argue about.

Lavinia is saying, "Nellie Bell, you're so openminded your brain fell out."

"Like all the other clichés and sound bites you speak in," Nell says, "that sounds cleverer than it is—even in an oversimplified way, but it's not true or even possible."

"You know what I mean by it, though, don't you?" Lavinia says. "To you everything is relative and everyone needs a hug, and everyone can be right at the same time. You have no mental and spiritual boundaries."

"And you have too many," she says. "You've limited yourself to only listening to people who agree with your worldview and confirm for you that you're right. You're too rigid and literal and believe that anyone who doesn't share your narrow, often hate-filled little bigoted beliefs is evil and going to hell."

"You don't even believe in hell—why does it matter to you if I think you're going there?"

Anna and I try to slip back out without being seen, but Lavinia motions me over to violate the six-feet rule and asks if I will check on Lillian.

9

———

Lillian is Lavinia's granddaughter, who she raised when her mother, Lily, was killed in a boating accident, and whose infant, Lilliana, had died a few months ago from a bacterial disease that she herself had survived.

Everything seemed fine at first. Lillian brought Lilliana home, and though Lillian had a cough that had been getting progressively worse since labor, Lilliana was happy and healthy. After a great first week, Lilliana began sneezing a little, and though she never really developed a cough, Lillian became convinced, based on her Google searches, that they had the whooping cough. Believed to be an overreacting new mother by her family and friends, Lillian took Lilliana to a walk-in clinic, where she was told everything was okay. Four days later, Lilliana began turning blue around her eyes because she wasn't getting enough oxygen. Eight days later, after heroic efforts by several specialists and following multiple seizures, Lilliana died in Lillian's arms.

I find her alone on the far corner of the back porch, silent tears trickling down her cheeks.

"I honestly thought I would've run out of tears by now," she says. "Sorry. I'm not doing this for show. I'm back here so no one will see me. I would've left but it seems to mean so much to Lavinia that I'm here that I just can't bring myself to do it. Instead I'm trying to pull myself together."

She is a younger, introverted version of Lavinia—every bit as regal and alluring, but in a far more subtle and quiet way.

"Mind if I join you?" I ask.

"No," she says. "Of course not. Please. Did she send you out to check on me?"

She didn't have to say who *she* is.

I nod, and take a seat farther away from her than I normally would. "I would have come out anyway if I had known you were here."

Extending down and out through a series of steps and platforms from the back porch, a slatted wooden dock, lined on either side by cypress trees, leads to a gazebo and boat shed in the river. The dock and the trees framing it are lit with small artistically arranged lights that cause it to look more like a Disney-designed resort than a private residence.

"Thank you again for checking on me the way you have—and for the . . . ah, memorial. You did such a beautiful job. Still don't see how you did it. But we all agreed it was perfect—and under the most impossible of circumstances."

"I was honored, just wish it was something that never had to be done."

Unlike the dock and the gnarled cypress trees surrounding it, the Apalachicola River isn't lit and can't be seen, but its presence is no less palpable for all that. It can be felt in the hushed, soothing spiritual aura of its serpentine mysteriousness and the gentle, disembodied slaps and splashes it makes.

She looks directly at me for the first time and locks her eyes onto mine. "Do you think some families are cursed?"

I shake my head. "I know it seems that way sometimes."

"You know a lot of people, have worked with a lot of wounded and grieving families—ever known someone who lost her mother as a child and her child as a mother?"

My eyes begin to sting, and as I blink, small tears pop out onto my face.

"I'm so, so sorry for all you've been through," I say. "I can see why it would seem like you're—"

"And it's not just me," she says, "my poor grandmother is shattered. She puts up a good front, but behind her facade it's only broken pieces. Nell's always been the craziest Tupelo Queen, but now Grandma may have her beat. It's hard to . . . believe, but . . . it may be even harder on her than me. They say seeing your child go through something hurts worse than you going through it. I . . . even for as short a time as I was a mother . . . I know it's true. I see . . . I see so many young mothers who neglect or ignore or complain about their babies, so many children disrespecting their mothers—or taking them for granted. I know you know what it's like to lose a mother, but that was as an adult and . . . prepared."

As a child, I had lost my mother into the black hole of alcoholism. As young man in Atlanta I had lost what felt like my wife and child in a traumatic fashion that I will forever associate with the Atlanta Child Murders. Since then I had undergone losses too numerous to name—including the actual death of my mother and losing my daughter, Johanna, for the first four years of her life. I understand loss. I've experienced grief so crushing I didn't think I would survive. But, of course, none of that is relevant to her particular pain, and I don't mention any of it.

"I'm okay," she adds. "I really am. I just don't need to be here. Could you let Grandma know I left and explain to her why it's okay that I did?"

"You sure you're okay?" I ask. "Ann and I can go with you or you can come to our place."

"I really am okay. I'm just not ready to be around people yet. I promise I'll call if I need anything—and you know I will. I've done it enough lately."

10

When I step back inside, I run into Jules in the large, open kitchen.

"How's the birthday girl holding up? Enjoying yourself?"

The kitchen is far more crowded than it would be if the guests and workers were following Zaire's recommendations. Attendees mill around, standing far too close to one another, as servers buzz about returning empty trays and trash, refilling, and returning to the fray.

"I'm happier'n a dead pig in the sunshine," she says. "Thank you ever so much for coming."

Mama Monroe, Merrill's mom and one of my surrogate mothers, is among the cooks preparing food, and she waves to me from the corner where she is slicing a huge ham.

To my surprise, the caterer is Dixie Ledoux, a classmate of the Tupelo Queens who also sings and acts, and has always seemed resentful of their talent, achievement, and popularity.

"I was shocked to see Tom and Randal," I say.

"*You* were?" she says. "I felt like someone slapped me upside the head and called me silly. Never been so flabbergasted in my entire life. But they're being on their best behavior—even brought me an expensive bottle of champagne."

"Almost as surprised as seeing you hired Dixie Ledoux to do your catering," I say quietly.

"Bless her heart," she whispers. "Won't make her hate us any less, but it will keep her business afloat for a few more months."

"You're a good a good man, Charlie Brown," I say.

"'Thou preparest a table before me in the presence of mine enemies,'" she says. "Speaking of . . . Did you see who else had the balls to deign to appear on my doorstep?"

"Who's that?" I say. "Max Reynolds?"

Lavinia's most recent husband Max seems to resent the Queens almost as much as Dixie Ledoux does, and he has never attended a single social function the Queens have been involved in.

"No, but his presence is a bit surprising given his disdain for us and, based on some of Lavinia's comments, that it's over between them. Of course, that's probably why he's here—trying to keep Lavinia from leaving him destitute. All the money is hers and they signed a prenup. She leaves him, he won't have a pot to piss in or a window to throw it out of—and you know his type is too poor to paint, too proud to whitewash. But no, I meant Sue Ann Gibson, the little hootch who stole Carson away from Nellie Bell. And what she's wearing . . . Her damn dress is so tight you can see her religion."

"She may be here to see if Nell will take Carson back," I say.

She lets out a loud burst of laughter at that. "Wouldn't that just beat all?"

As Nash, Harley, and Jasmine walk up, Jules says, "Well, I've got to go herd the cats for our performance. See you all in the theater in a few. Thanks again for coming."

We wish her well and I turn my attention to Nash, Jasmine, and Harley. Paul is conspicuously missing.

"I was hoping to see you tonight," I say to Nash. "How's it going?"

He nods. "Okay."

"A lot better now," Jasmine says. "Paul and I are on a break."

"How are you?" I ask her.

"It wasn't easy," she says. "I really care about him, but—" she pats Nash on the shoulder "—can't have anyone putting his hands on my boy."

"You've got a great son," I say, then to him and Harley, "And you guys obviously have a great mom."

They all nod and express their agreement.

"Were you talking to Lillian out there?" Jasmine asks.

I nod.

"I feel so bad for her," she says. "I just . . . don't know what to do for her. I've reached out a few times, but she really hasn't responded. We grew up in different towns and were never close as kids. I was just getting to know her as an adult—actually hanging out on our own some and not just at these Queen events when it happened. If you can think of anything I can do for her . . ."

"I will," I say. "Keep reaching out to her."

"Thanks, I will."

"The reason I wanted to see you," I say to Nash, "is I remember you mentioning you were interested in learning to play an instrument a while back."

"Yeah?"

"I bought a guitar during a case I was working last year that I'd like you to have," I say. "It's new—still in the box. I haven't even taken it out. I don't have time to learn it, so it's yours if you want it."

"Cool," Nash says. "Thanks."

"Yes, thank you, John," Jasmine says. "That's . . ."

We come up with a plan to get Nash the guitar, our conversation wanes, and we drift in different directions.

11

———

I grab a bottle of water from the ice-filled number 3 washtub on the floor and go in search of Anna.

Passing Carla, who is talking to the Foster brothers in the hallway, I ask if she has seen her, and she directs me to the dining room.

I find Anna standing with Merrill and Zaire listening to Nellie and Lavinia continue to go at it.

"How'd it go?" Anna asks.

I shrug. "Okay, I guess. She went home. I'd like for us to ride by and check on her when we leave here."

"We can go by and see her and check on John Paul if we leave pretty soon."

"Yeah," Merrill says, "we need to do that too."

"What?" Zaire asks.

"Check on people—shit, anything that gets us out of here sooner."

"At least I don't live in fear and broker in conspiracy theory nonsense," Nell is saying. "What is it this week? 5G? Deep state? Chem trails? Coronavirus hoax?"

Lavinia is about to respond when Jules walks in and interrupts. "Careful there, Nellie Bell," she says. "Lavinia's got more than her fair share of crazy theories, but you've got a few of your own."

"Such as?"

"Body earthing, essential oils, anti-vaxing, aromatherapy, some questionable Eastern philosophies, the essential, innate goodness of everyone, spirit animals, runes, enneagrams, crystals," she says.

Lavinia starts to say something but stops, and an awkward moment ensues.

Jules says to the small, suddenly quiet crowd, "It's almost time for the champagne toast and special Tupelo Queens surprise performance. Everyone please make your way to the Tupelo Theater."

As we start to drift toward the theater with the rest of the herd, Merrill says, "Now be a good time for us to slip out."

Zaire says, "And miss the chance to hear these old white women argue some more?" She glances at me. "No offense, but your aunt's friends are a little nuts. They really believe all that shit—all those complicated and convoluted conspiracy theories, that flat earth, birther bullshit? And what about the coronavirus being a hoax and not vaccinating their kids?"

"Evidently," I say. "Hadn't heard some of that. It's interesting that they're on opposite ends of the political spectrum but both believe similarly wacky nonsense. It's ironic to think about . . . If Lavinia truly believes the virus is a hoax and Nell's truly an anti-vaxer, will they both not get a COVID-19 shot once we have one, but for very different reasons?"

"You know what it all means?" Merrill says. "Now be a good time for us to go."

12

The small, plush theater is a good bit cooler than the rest of Jules's home, and even with the house lights on has a different look, feel, and vibe.

Seating is even more limited than usual because of the number of seats taped off in order to keep attendees as separated as possible.

After flashing twice, the house lights fade, and a spotlight illuminates the center of the curtain now rising to reveal the Tupelo Queens dressed as the Andrew Sisters in faux retro World War II military uniforms.

Following a big salute to the audience, they begin choreographed, synchronized dance moves, while snapping their fingers and singing Leslie Gore's "It's My Party."

Moving and sounding nearly as good as they ever did, it's impressive to see these older women display so much energy, poise, agility.

"It's My Party" fades into Destiny's Child's "Birthday," and the soft, smooth strings not only offer a nice contrast to the previous song, but show off the Queens' amazing harmonies.

This is followed by Neil Sedaka's "Happy Birthday Sweet Sixteen" and then the Beatles' "Birthday."

It's obvious all three women are born entertainers and are enjoying themselves.

The final two songs of the medley are genuinely surprising and hilarious, and we all respond like the Queens no doubt wanted us to.

Striking rapper stances, these aging white ladies begin to move like fly girls in classic hip-hop videos and begin to rap 50 Cent's "Go Shorty" like old pros.

Loud cheers, screams, whistles, and uproarious laughter emanate from the increasingly raucous crowd.

But none of this compares to the next level pandemonium that occurs when "Go Shorty" fades and they begin Jeremih's "Birthday Sex."

A lengthy and enthusiastic standing ovation follows the energetic, entertaining, and unexpected performance, all three breathless and sweating Queens soaking it in.

"And now," Nell says, "let's raise a glass to the Queen of the hour."

Carla rolls a cart holding a bottle of champagne and three glasses onto the stage. As Nell pops the top and pours the Queens generous portions into their glasses, Carla joins the other servers who pop corks, pour, and pass out glasses to the still standing audience.

"To Queen Jules," Nell says, beginning to slur her words, her glass held high beginning to shake. "May you live to be so old you're wrinkled, toothless, bald, hunched, and unrecogni . . ."

"In other words," Lavinia adds, slurring her words as well, "at least another day or . . ."

"To Jules," Nell says. "Happy Birth . . ."

Everyone repeats "Happy Birthday" and takes a drink of their champagne.

"Many happy re—" Lavinia says, looking alarmed that she's losing the capacity of speech.

Jules starts to say something, but suddenly passes out, folding onto the floor.

At first everyone seems to think she's playing, but within a few seconds, Nell and Lavinia are doing the same thing.

In moments all three women are unconscious on the floor.

In another moment, Merrill, Zaire, Anna, and I are on the stage, Dad following close behind, calling for backup and emergency services as he does.

Zaire yells for someone to call for ambulances, then says to us. "A toxicologist will have to confirm it, but I'm pretty sure they've been poisoned."

13

───────

"John, I didn't have anything to do with what happened," Carla is saying.

"What do you mean?"

"I mean . . . I . . . People are sayin' they were poisoned. If they were . . . I didn't have anything to do with it. Everything that happened was an accident and I was just doing what I was told."

"What was an accident?" I ask. "What happened?"

We are in the parlor, seated not far from the table where Jules's presents remain unopened.

Jules's house is largely empty now, most of the attendees allowed to leave after giving their names, addresses, and statements to Dad and his deputies. Most of the staff remain behind. The FDLE crime scene investigation unit has just arrived and are processing the place, including the bottle of champagne and three glasses used on stage by the Tupelo Queens, which we had bagged the moment Zaire mentioned they may have been poisoned.

Zaire rode in the ambulance with Jules and Lavinia. Verna

and Jasmine rode with Nell. We're waiting for word on their condition and what the initial drug screening shows.

Anna is at our house with Nash, Harley, John Paul, Johanna, and Taylor.

Merrill had gone to pick up Lillian and take her to the hospital to see her grandmother and should be back soon.

"In addition to my other duties, I was given the assignment to roll the cart with the champagne and glasses on it on stage. It was like this big honor or something—some of the other servers seemed jealous. I didn't see it as anything to get bent out of shape over. It just seemed like more work, more responsibility to me—and I just didn't want to screw it up. But that's exactly what I did."

"How?"

"We kept the cart with all the stuff—the ice bucket with the ice and champagne in it and the glasses—in the small dressing room backstage of the theater. When it was almost time for the show to start, I went back there to check on everything and get ready and . . . when I lifted the bottle out of the bucket to see if it was chilled enough, I . . . it was wet and slippery and I dropped it. The bottle didn't break or anything, but the cork hit the side of the cart and popped off and opened and spilled everywhere. I freaked out. I didn't know what to do. I knew they wanted to pop the top on the stage and pour their own drinks—they have so many little traditions like that—so I couldn't just bring out an open bottle and glasses with the champagne already in them. I . . . I decided the only thing I could do was to go and tell Miss Dixie what had happened and ask her what I should do, but on the way I remembered that someone had given Miss Jules a bottle of champagne for her birthday, so I dashed in here and grabbed it."

I glance over at the gift table to see that the bottle of champagne the Foster brothers had given Jules is gone.

"And I just took it back and replaced it," she says. "That's all

I did. I swear. I knew it wouldn't be chilled enough, but I stuck it in the ice bucket so it could be in there as long as possible before time to roll it out on stage. I figured afterwards they'd complain about it being too warm, but I didn't know what else to do. And then . . . someone said they were poisoned . . . so I just wanted you to know if they were, I didn't have anything to do with it."

"What were Tom and Randal talking to you about in the hallway before everyone went into the theater?" I ask.

She shrugs and twists her lips into a little frown. "Nothing really . . . just sort of hittin' on me and kind of offerin' me a job at the same time."

"Did they mention the champagne or anything related to it?"

"Not that I can remember," she says. "They may've mentioned champagne, but not anything to do with tonight or Jules or the bottle they brought."

"Then what?"

"I wasn't really paying attention, but one of them said something about keepin' their women in caviar and champagne or something like that."

"As a way of reminding you about the bottle they brought without coming out and saying it directly?" I say, wondering aloud.

14

When Merrill arrives a short while later, he motions me and Dad out onto the front porch.

"Za just called as I was pulling up," he says. "She was right. Drug screening the ER did shows they had oxycodone poisoning."

"They gonna be okay?" I ask.

"Says so. Guess I shoulda led with that."

"All three were poisoned in the same manner?" I ask.

He nods. "All three and all three with oxycodone."

"And all right in front of us," Dad says.

"It's embarrassing," I say.

"Killer got some stones on him," Merrill says.

"How do you even get poison into an uncorked champagne bottle?" Dad says.

"Turns out we've got far more to answer than just that," I say.

"Whatta you mean?"

"The bottle they were supposed to drink from was broken and a substitute bottle was used—but it was done in such a way that it's hard to see how anyone could've predicted that particular bottle would be the one used."

I tell them what Carla told me.

"Oh, no," Dad says.

"Oh, *hell yes*," Merrill says. "I can tell already . . . this case gonna be a John Jordan special."

"I don't know," I say. "You've been solvin' as many as me lately. Maybe more."

"Not this Colonel Mustard in the theater with the champagne shit," he says. "That's all your Hercule Holmes Father Brown ass. You just better hurry 'fore the pandemic wipes us all out."

15

"This a residence or a pharmacy?" Russel Walters says.

He's a tall, long-faced, black-bearded crime scene tech with FDLE, still in his bunny suit, though the hood is down and his face is uncovered. Based on the way he's speaking and acting, I'm guessing he's unaware this is Dad's sister's home.

"She cared for a terminally ill husband until about six months ago," Dad says.

I can hear the defensiveness in his voice, but it's subtle and I doubt Russel can.

We're standing in Jules's master suit, which is enormous and extravagant, and it feels like a violation to be here.

Dad, Gerald Woodson—the investigator Dad has assigned to the case—Merrill, and I are standing with Russel in a large open area between Jules's California king and her huge antique vanity. Through the open bathroom door, we can see the two female techs finishing bagging and tagging the last of the items from the medicine cabinet.

"Well, evidently she didn't flush his meds when he passed."

"Did you find oxycodone or not?" Dad asks, his irritation rising to the surface.

Russel stares at Dad for a moment, seemingly trying to decide whether or not to react to Dad's shortness. Finally, he just nods slowly and says, "I was coming to that. Yes, we found a great deal of it—including some in liquid form that would be easier to introduce into a drink. I understand that's the theory —that someone spiked the champagne."

"Possibly," I say. "It's also possible the bottle was already spiked and nothing from here was used."

"Well, we'll get everything tested and see what we come up with," he says. "We've got the glasses, the bottle, the cork, samples of the drinks and food that were served, the meds, but my guess is it came from the bottle of liquid oxycodone we found."

"Why is that?" Dad asks.

"Two things," he says. "Based on the dust on the shelf and the meds and the lack of it where the bottle had been, I'd say the bottle was moved recently, perhaps tonight, *and* . . . the fact that it has been wiped clean. It's the only bottle—hell, maybe even the only surface—in the entire house that doesn't have a single print on it."

"Interesting," I say. "And there's enough missing from it for it to have been used?"

He nods, his hood waving up and down as he does. "And then some."

"Find anything else suspicious?" Dad asks.

"No, not really," he says. "Something could show up upon further analysis or in tox screenings, but everything else appears pretty typical—given there was a party here tonight."

"Thanks," Dad says. "Please rush everything you can and have the lab do the same."

"Will do. We're almost done. Just a few more minutes and we'll be out of here."

He then turns and joins the other two techs in the bathroom.

"If he's right," I say after he's gone, "and the bottle of liquid oxycodone he recovered is the source of the poison given to the Queens, then it probably wasn't the Foster brothers."

Dad nods. "True. They would've brought it already laced with the poison, not injected into the bottle once they got here."

"Yeah, I'd say if what was used to poison them came from the house—whether it's the liquid oxy he found or not—that tells us something about the nature of the attempted murder and maybe even the would-be murderer."

"What's that?" Dad says. "And are we for sure saying it couldn't've been some kind of freak accident?"

"Don't think we can rule out anything yet," I say, "but it's hard to see how it could be an accident. If it was attempted murder, then . . . grabbing something here and using it shows lack of planning, indicates it was a crime of opportunity. Spur of the moment. Off the cuff. Could've been something said or done at the party set him or her off."

"True," Dad says.

"What I want to know," Merrill says, "whether it was brought that way or put in once it got here . . . is how the hell you get poison into a sealed bottle of champagne to begin with?"

16

———

"Still can't believe we were poisoned," Jules is saying. "*Poisoned.*"

"We think so," I say. "It's at least possible it was some sort of accident. We won't know for sure until the lab results come back and we know more. But it's hard to see how it could be anything but a deliberate attempt on your lives."

"After all we've been through this year," Lavinia says.

Dad, Gerald Woodson, and I are at Sacred Heart in Port St. Joe, where Zaire has worked it out for Nell and Lavinia to be rolled down in wheelchairs to Jules's room so we can talk to all three of them at once.

"Our biggest concern was spreading the virus," Nell says.

"Can y'all think of anyone who'd do something like this?" Woodson asks.

They all nod.

"Sure," Lavinia says.

"We all have our enemies," Nell says.

"We can each come up with people who wish we were dead," Jules says. "My stepsons, Lavinia's soon-to-be ex. Nell's—I'm not sure anyone would want to hurt Nell. If we search hard enough, I'm sure we could find someone who'd like for Nell to shuffle off her mortal coil. But that's the thing. We can come up with people who want us dead—as individuals—but not as a group. I can't think of anyone who'd try to kill us all—or any reason someone could possibly have. *Unless*—" she grows animated, emphasizing that last word to set up what she's about to suggest "—it's another trio jealous of our talent, anxious to get us out of the way so they can finally have the spotlight."

"This is no joke, Jules," Dad says. "You were almost murdered tonight."

"I know—and on my damn birthday, but . . . if I don't find a little levity somewhere, I'm liable to curl up in a ball and cry myself silly."

I notice that under the stress of their current circumstance none of them use as many Southernisms—not even Jules who typically uses the most.

"We've got to consider the possibility that only one of you was the intended target," I say. "And that either the other two weren't meant to be poisoned or were considered acceptable collateral damage by the killer."

"We'll need a list of the people you think it's even possible could want you dead," Woodson says.

They nod and say they'll compile them.

"Some of our lists will be longer than others," Lavinia says. "My guess is mine'll be the longest and Nell's will be the shortest."

"Did the champagne taste funny or smell bad?" I ask. "Odd? Different in any way?"

They all think about it for a moment and each agree that it did not.

"It was a little on the warm side," Lavinia says. "Nearly room temperature. But I didn't notice anything odd about it other than that."

"Me either," Nell says.

"Agree," Jules adds.

"Nell," I say, "you popped the top and poured the three glasses, didn't you?"

She nods.

"Poured very generously I might add," Lavinia says.

"Not that we complained at the time," Jules says.

"Did you notice anything odd or off about the bottle or the glasses?" I ask.

She shakes her head. "Nothing that I noticed. But I really wasn't paying attention. I hadn't even planned on doing it—just sort of did."

"We had no set plan of who would do what," Lavinia says.

"Was there anything in the glasses before you poured into them?" I ask.

She shrugs. "Don't think so. If there was I didn't notice."

I say, "Did the three of you eat or drink any of the same things at any point throughout the night?"

They confer with each other for a few minutes, carefully going over everything, and determine that there wasn't.

"I don't think any of us ate or drank much of anything at all," Jules says. "We usually don't before a performance. And we certainly didn't all eat or drink the same things—let alone out of the same containers."

17

"Can I speak to you two for a minute?" Gerald Woodson says.

He, Dad, and I have just stepped out of the hospital into dark, late-night air.

We step over to the side away from the entrance, though no one is coming or going.

"I gotta have some clarification," he says.

"About?" Dad says.

"Is this my case or not?"

"Whatta you mean?" Dad says.

"I just need to know," he says. "I know you're new to the new department, and I didn't work for you before. But I'm a hell of an investigator when I'm allowed to do my job."

Dad nods. "I've heard good things about you."

"I could hardly get a question in in there," he says. "I realize he's your son and that he's actually a very good investigator, but that's in another county and—"

"I'm sorry," I say. "You're right. I overstepped my bounds in there. I should've let you take the lead and—"

"*Take the lead*?" he says. "You shouldn't've been in there at all. You're a witness in this case, not an investigator. I shouldn't have to fight for space and freedom to investigate in my own investigation."

"You're right," I say. "You shouldn't."

"I asked John to join us," Dad says.

"I know and I know he's your son and I know I'm risking my job here, but . . . well, I guess I don't want to work in a department that's run like a family business."

Dad nods. "I appreciate you speaking your mind," he says. "And you're damn sure not risking your job to do so. Makes me respect and trust you even more. The thing is though, I'd want John on an investigation even if we weren't related. He's the very best investigator I've ever come across in all my years. Someone tried to kill my sister tonight. I'm going to utilize every resource I have to find out who and make sure they don't succeed in a second attempt."

"That's the other thing, sir," he says. "Neither one of you should be involved in this case. It's a family member, for God sakes. If it were my sister or my aunt, would you let me within a mile of the investigation?"

Dad starts to say something, then stops, takes a deep breath and lets it out slowly before continuing. "Okay. I appreciate what you're saying and . . . you're not wrong. I do. It won't be a problem anymore. Run your investigation the way you want to. We won't interfere. John won't get in your way again, but family member or not, you're stuck with me. I want daily reports and I want to know any time a new development happens or a new lead emerges. It's my department, but it's your case. Just keep me informed and up to date. I want to be the first to know. Understand?"

He nods. "Understood."

"Okay," Dad says, "now go get some sleep so you'll be your best to start the investigation in the morning."

"Tomorrow's Sunday," he says.

"Actually, today is Sunday," Dad says. "Tomorrow is Monday. And I expect you to work them both to find out who's — You wanted this case all to yourself. Well, you got it. So work it."

"Yes, sir," he says, nodding vigorously. Turning to me, he extends his hand and says, "No hard feelings. Nothing personal. Just trying to do my job and I'm going to do a good job for y'all."

"Thank you," I say, shaking his hand.

As he turns and makes his way to his vehicle across the way in the dim, empty parking lot, Dad and I head for my truck.

As Woodson pulls away, Dad says, "Give him plenty of space. Stay away from him. But whatever you do, don't stop investigating. Someone tried to kill my own sister right in front of me tonight, and I want his ass. Or hers."

"I won't stop until we have his or her ass."

SUNDAY, MARCH 15, 2020

Sunday, March 15, 2020
3,501 confirmed cases and 56 deaths in the US

The CDC recommends that people in the US not gather in groups of fifty or more for the next eight weeks, including birthday parties, weddings, music festivals, spring city festivals, parades, concerts, sporting events, and conferences.

"Younger people should be concerned for two reasons," Dr. Fauci says. "You are not immune or safe from getting seriously ill. Even though when you look at the total numbers, it's overwhelmingly weighted toward the elderly and those with underlying conditions. But the virus isn't a mathematical formula. There are going to be people who are young who are going to wind up getting seriously ill. So protect yourself, but remember that you can also be a vector or a carrier. And even though you don't get seriously ill, you could bring it to a person, who could bring it to a person, that would bring it to your grandfather, your grandmother or your elderly relative. That's why everybody has to take this seriously, even the young."

18

"They really did a number on the joint, didn't they?" Jules is saying. "Makes my ass itch."

She and I are back at her place doing a walk-through following her release from the hospital the afternoon of the next day.

Pausing in the foyer, we take it all in.

She glances to the left, through the open French doors into the parlor at all the gifts and smiles, then to the den on the right and frowns and shakes her head.

Her plush, spacious home looks to have hosted a party the night before that had yet to be cleaned up from, followed hard on by a herd of cops and forensic techs tromping through it.

Abandoned trays of wine and hors d'oeuvres lie about. Discarded dessert plates with remnants of food and wadded napkins on them and empty and near-empty wine glasses litter the once immaculate landscape.

"Mama Monroe, bless her, said she'd come help me clean it," she says. "And I could use it. My old ass needs all the help it can get—'specially on the domestic front. 'Course she's no spring chicken herself, but she can outwork a worn-in tractor."

"And you have no idea who could've been behind it?" I ask.

"The mess?" she says. "Sure, the damn cops. My brother's own department, and they trash it like they're serving a warrant at a meth house."

"Not the mess," I say. "The attempted murder."

"No, but I want to figure it out before you do," she says.

"Oh yeah?"

"You know you're not the only detective in the family, don't you?" she says. "I've solved a few cases in my day. I know Jack's a sheriff and all—and a damn good one—but I've always thought you got some of your detecting skills from me."

"I'm sure I did."

"Speaking of," she says, "I'd like to work with you on this one. Someone tried to kill me and my oldest, dearest friends and I take that very personally. Was thinking we could work it together and see who figures it out first."

"I'm not working it," I say. "Gerald Woodson of the Potter County Sheriff's Department is."

"Well, can I not work it with you?"

"I can't stop you from not working it," I say.

"Splendid."

We walk down the wide hardwood hallway beside the large African mahogany staircase toward the kitchen in the back of the house, passing random dust swirls of black fingerprinting powder on various surfaces as we do.

"Do you think the Foster boys could be behind it?" I ask.

She shakes her head. "They'd rob me blind if they could, but I don't think they're capable of murder. Hellfire, I've got at least my big toe in the grave already. Maybe more. All they've got to do is show a little patience."

"That's not something they're known for, is it?"

"Guess you got a point there."

We step into the kitchen and pause.

Stacks and stacks of serving trays and pots and pans, most

with food still on them, are piled everywhere—next to and in between bags and boxes, knives and spoons, cutting boards and preparing stations.

It looks like the kitchen in a large metropolitan hotel following a fire alarm for a bomb threat, after which no one was allowed back inside for days.

"Ain't nothin' get my knickers in a knot faster than this," she says. "Not just the wreck and ruin and rot, but the waste."

"We'll call for backup and help you get it cleaned up and squared away. Does the money go to the brothers when you shimmy and shake and soft-shoe off your mortal coil?"

"Unless I change my will."

"Could they be afraid you're going to?"

"Crazy old woman like me, wouldn't you be?"

"So they have motive?"

"*Oh*, they *have* motive," she says. "About 4.4 million of them. But I've assured them I'm leaving the bulk of the estate to them, and they're about the least violent boys you're likely ever to meet."

"And poisoning is about the least violent method of murder *you're* likely ever to meet."

"Well, now, there is that. Okay, so we don't cross them off the suspect list just yet."

"You have a suspect list?" I ask.

"How else 'm I gonna beat you at this?"

"Who else is on it?"

"No one," she says. "The boys weren't on it until you put them there. I genuinely don't know anyone who'd want to murder us. Who'd want to kill a bunch of little old ladies? Seriously? I just don't think I know any honest to God cold-blooded killers."

"You know more than you think you do," I say.

"I guess I must, because I don't think I know any."

"How about Dixie?" I ask.

She looks shocked as she looks from me to the far corner of the kitchen where the night before Dixie Ledoux had been overseeing everything. "She's resented us for decades. Why kill us now? We give her work."

"Maybe that's why," I say. "She feels like you're flaunting it —throwing your wonderful lives in her face."

"Our *wonderful* lives?" she says. "Husbands and great-grand-babies dying. Divorces. Sicknesses. Mastectomies. Disasters. Bankruptcy."

"I'm sure she has all that on top of not getting to be one of you. Tell me about the disasters and bankruptcies."

"You know," she says, "Hurricane Michael all but leveled Nellie Bell's place in Wewa. Not sure if she was un- or underin-sured, but she's destitute. Lavinia and I have become her patrons."

"And the mastectomies and sicknesses?"

"First one then the other," she says. "Both of Lavinia's over-the-shoulder boulder holders are now empty—well . . . padded with some sort of jelly filled rubber tits, complete with color-less nipples and all. And you know all too well about her great-grandbaby. Nellie Bell's husband just left her and it looks like Lavinia's is about to do the same."

"Thought she was leaving him?"

"Well, yeah, I guess, but the misery and messiness of it is all the same, matters not who's leaving whom."

"True," I say, "but it matters greatly when it comes to motives for murder."

"Now you're talkin' some sense, boy," she says. "Definitely put Max's mean 'ol wacky wingnut ass on the suspect list."

"And the sicknesses?" I ask.

"Well, at our age . . ." she says. "We keep some sort of illness almost all the time, but I guess I was speaking specifically of poor Nellie Bell. She's been sick as a dog since she's been back from her post-divorce cruise. She's doin' better now, bless her heart, but we weren't sure she was gonna make it there for a while."

"What was it?" I ask. "Was she tested for the coronavirus? Lot of people on cruise ships getting infected."

"I doubt it," she says. "She's an old hippie. Probably just rubbed some herbs and essential oils on her tits and burned some sage or something. Don't think she'd go to the doctor even if she could afford it. Besides . . . she's better now. Whatever she had is long gone."

"We need to get her tested," I say.

"Are there any of the dern tests available yet?"

"Some," I say. "We need to see if she had it and who all she could've exposed."

"She's been back a little over two weeks. Didn't leave her house until a few days ago—except to go to yours to meet with Zaire. Made all of us drop off the groceries and stuff we took her on the porch. Whatever she had . . . she didn't give it to anyone else."

"We need to know for sure," I say.

We fall quiet a beat and she seems miles away for a moment.

Eventually, she turns to me and says, "I can't stay in this filthy kitchen another second."

"Let's go to the master suite," I say. "I have some questions for you."

"Okay," she says, and begins to move slowly in that direction. "Is it possible it was an accident?"

"Don't really see how it could be," I say.

"Could it have been intended for someone else—in the audience maybe."

"Didn't the audience have a different type of champagne than y'all?"

"Oh, well, yeah. We always buy the best for our toast and

some that's . . . let's just say a little *less* expensive for everyone else."

"So it's hard to see how it could've been meant for anyone but y'all."

As we approach the medicine cabinet, which is actually a small closet, I ask her about Randall Foster, Sr.'s illness and prescriptions.

"His particular form of bone cancer was excruciatingly painful," she says. "He wanted to be at home, to die at home, so with the help of home health and hospice I gave him what he wanted. It was like we were running a small hospital with a patient of one—complete with our own pharmacy. I kept meaning to flush all his meds, but . . . just never got around to it. To be honest I avoided it, just didn't want to deal with it. Still haven't touched a single thing of his—not his clothes, his guns, his tools, nothing. Just haven't been able to bring myself to do it."

Looking at the empty fingerprint-dust-covered closet, she adds, "Guess this was one way to get it done."

"I know it's hard to see with all the fingerprint powder, but do you see this spot here?"

I point to one of the many small circular patterns in the dust on the top shelf.

She nods.

"The bottle that caused that mark there is the only one that wasn't in its spot," I say. "It has been moved recently and not returned to the exact same spot it had been in. Do you recall moving it at any time for anything?"

She shakes her head. "What was it?"

I show her a picture of the bottle of liquid oxycodone.

Her eyes widen. "That's it?" she says. "That's what was used on us?"

"We don't know for sure," I say, "and won't until toxicology comes back—but it's the only one that has been moved and wiped down recently."

"Wiped down?" she says. "There are no prints on it?"

"None whatsoever," I say.

"Well, that's it," she says. "That's the weapon someone used to try to kill us. Has to be. It should have my prints on it—I gave a dose to Ron right before he died. Haven't touched it since then—so it should've still been in its little dust circle, which I'm mortified is there, by the way. And in addition to all that, there was a lot more in that little bottle the last time I saw it. It was nearly full."

MONDAY, MARCH 16, 2020

Monday, March 16, 2020
4,373 confirmed cases and 76 deaths in the US

The following day, the CDC recommends US citizens avoid gathering in groups of more than ten.

EXECUTIVE ORDER

Tuesday, March 17, 2020

GOVERNOR ISSUED EXECUTIVE ORDER REGARDING BARS, BEACHES AND RESTAURANTS

On March 17, Governor Ron DeSantis issued an executive order that will reduce density and crowds in restaurants, bars, nightclubs and beaches to mitigate the spread of coronavirus (COVID-19).

BARS AND NIGHTCLUBS

Under the direction of Governor DeSantis, all bars and nightclubs throughout Florida will close for the next thirty days. Department of Business and Professional Regulation (DBPR) will be enforcing and providing further guidance.

BEACHES

The governor is directing parties accessing public beaches in the state of Florida to follow the Centers for Disease Control and Prevention (CDC) guidance by limiting their gatherings to no more than ten persons, distancing themselves from other parties by six feet.

RESTAURANTS

Restaurants across the state of Florida will now be required to limit customer entry to 50 percent of capacity. Seating must be staggered and limited to ensure seated parties are separated by a distance of at least six feet, in accordance with CDC guidelines. Restaurants are encouraged to remain open and expand take-out and delivery services. Additional information will be provided by DBPR.

MASS GATHERINGS

Continue to follow information from the CDC on mass gatherings. CDC, in accordance with its guidance for large events and mass gatherings, recommends that for the next eight weeks, organizers (whether groups or individuals) cancel or postpone in-person events that consist of ten people or more throughout the United States. This recommendation is made in an attempt to reduce introduction of the virus into new communities and to slow the spread of infection in communities already affected by the virus.

TESTING

Call your health care provider first if you are symptomatic to determine the need for testing. If a person thinks they have COVID-19, they should call their health care provider before going to their office so the provider can take precautions to prevent exposing other people. In some cases, they are going to meet you in the parking lot. It's just a precaution. We are really trying to keep our health care workers safe. Other patients safe. Review your signs, symptoms, and travel history with your physician. Your physician will evaluate you for other possible causes of respiratory illness and also contact the county health department to coordinate COVID-19 testing.

- To be prioritized for testing, patients must meet the state's criteria, which evaluates a combination of symptoms and risk factors. Their samples will be sent to the closest laboratory.

- If you don't meet priority criteria, you can discuss with

your provider about possibly getting tested at a commercial laboratory (e.g. LabCorp or Quest).

·   State lab results are generally available within twenty-four to forty-eight hours. Commercial labs can take three to four days. Turnaround time can for all be affected by demand.

CLOSURES

All schools will be closed until April 15. The district is working on an Instructional Continuity Plan for home-based learning until schools reopen. This plan will be implemented on Monday, March 30. Details will be released later this week, along with details for the student feeding program.

All government buildings will be closed to the public effective at the close of business on March 18. You may reach any department by telephone or email.

19

———

"By following your recommendations," Jules is saying, glancing over her shoulder at Zaire, "we did at my party what the country is doing now."

It's Thursday and we're back in Jules's theater, each of us sitting several seats apart from the others, waiting as Zaire prepares everything up on the stage. Jules is down front in between the first row of chairs and the stage.

"I wish the country was doing it," Zaire says. "Far too many are not—and it should've been implemented weeks ago."

"Of course," she says. "I just wanted you to know I appreciate you and I feel good that we did our part—that we're still doing our part."

Still doing our part, we are in a small group and remaining a minimum of six feet away from each other. We're also wearing masks—an additional precaution Zaire and not our local, state, or federal elected officials recommended.

"You'll all be happy to know that everything in the house has been scrubbed from the rootie to the tootie," Jules adds, "including our disgusting vomit and other such vileness that would knock a buzzard off a gut wagon from the stage you're about to walk across. I want to thank all y'all again for the wonderful birthday and say again how sorry I am that I almost got my best friends killed."

Zaire finishes her preparation and Jules turns the floor over to her.

"Okay," she says. "The test I'm gonna give you today is a nasal swab. It's uncomfortable and may hurt a little, but it's not too bad. I'll have you come up one at a time, entering the stage to my left, your right, and exiting to my right and your left. I should have the results back to you within a day or so, but it's important to remember that the only thing this test can tell us is if you currently have the virus. It won't let me know if you've ever had it and it gives no indication of if you might get it. Unfortunately, it's all we can do right now. Contrary to what some are saying and others are reporting, tests aren't yet readily available."

When Jules told Nell she thought she should be tested, she said she would only do it if she wasn't the only one. Jules and Lavinia agreed to be tested as well, and since Zaire was going to come to Jules's to administer the tests anyway, she offered to test anyone from the party who wanted to come, though she insisted everyone sign up ahead of time and come in shifts in groups of no more than ten.

This current group included Jules, Nell and Jasmine, Lavinia and Lillian, me and Anna, Carla, Dixie Ledoux, and Dad.

Verna is home watching the children—Johanna, Taylor, John Paul, Harley, Nash—but Zaire has already tested her, along with Merrill and Mama Monroe.

"Okay if we talk?" Lavinia asks.

"Won't bother me any, if that's what you mean," Zaire says.

Lavinia turns and looks over from Jules to Dad and then me. "Can we talk about what happened?" she asks.

"We'll talk about anything you want to, dear," Jules says.

"Well," Lavinia says, "what the hell happened? Did someone really try to kill us? And if so, who—and while we're at it, how and why?"

Dad clears his throat and slides forward in his seat. "We do believe y'all were intentionally poisoned. We believe the *how* to be in your champagne, but we won't know for sure until we get the toxicology results back from the lab—and those take a while. We're investigating the *who* and the *why*—which are often discovered together."

Jules turns in her chair and looks back toward us. "And they think the poison used was some of Ron's own supply left over from his illness that I hadn't poured out yet."

"It just doesn't seem possible," Lavinia says. "Who in the Sam Hill would want us dead?"

"Anyone who's been subjected to our singing for the past several decades," Nell says. "Got to be a long list."

"You think this is funny?" Lavinia says, her voice filled with equal parts fear and anger.

"Nobody thinks it's funny, dear," Jules says. "Saying inappropriate shit is how we've always dealt with intense and uncomfortable situations. No need to get you knickers in a knot over it now."

"*Someone tried to kill us*," Lavinia says, slowly enunciating every syllable. "It's got to be some sort of mistake. Just hearing myself say it out loud like that . . . It's ludicrous. Who'd want to kill harmless old ladies who'll be dead soon anyway? Is it even safe for us to be here now?"

"It is," Dad says. "John and I are both armed."

"So am I," Lavinia says. "And was the night of the party— and a lot of good that did us."

"If you don't feel safe, dear—"

"The cork popped," Lavinia says.

"Huh?" Jules asks.

"The champagne bottle," she says. "The cork popped. The

seal hadn't been broken. How do you get poison into a champagne bottle without breaking the seal?" She turns toward Nell, who is seated on the opposite side of the theater. "Are you sure there wasn't anything in those glasses?"

"Pretty sure," she says.

Carla clears her throat. "The glasses were empty. I polished them again just before I rolled the cart onto the stage."

"No offense," Lavinia says, "but we only have your word for that." Turning to Dad she asks, "Is she a suspect? Are you looking at her?"

"We're looking at everybody," he says.

She turns back toward the stage. "What if the swab is poisoned?"

Dixie Ledoux, who is being tested, jerks her head back and away from the long nasal swab in her right nostril.

Zaire turns, her frustration and anger palpable, and slowly says, "The swabs aren't poisoned. They are factory sealed—"

"So was the champagne."

"Lavinia," Jules says, her voice firm. "You don't have to take the test. You don't even have to be here."

"I know that, but it's not like I feel any safer anywhere else."

"We're all scared," Nell says. "But Jules or her brother or nephew will figure it out. I'm sure there's a simple explanation —whether the poison was intended for us or not."

"You're right," Lavinia says. "They probably will, but you tell me how we stay alive and keep from going crazy between now and then."

W

"What I'd like to do is start from when you two were talking in here and Jules came to the door and said it was almost time for the toast," I say.

Anna, Carla, and I are in the den with Jules, Lavinia, and Nell.

Dixie is in the kitchen. Dad is in the hallway. The others have gone.

"It'd be helpful for us to know your movements between here and there, who you saw, what you heard, if you remember anyone or anything being suspicious."

"Okay," Jules says. "I was in the kitchen sort of checking on everything—saw you when you came in from talking to poor Lilly—and a little while later I realized what time it was, so I came down the hallway to the doorway here, caught the tail end of their little tête-à-tête and told everyone it was about time to gather in the theater."

"Then what'd you do?" I ask.

"Then I made my way to the theater," she says. "I was stopped several times—by friends giving me birthday greetings or the staff asking questions—so much so that I was the last to arrive in our dressing room. Oh, and I went wee on the way too."

"We all did that," Nell says.

"We always do," Lavinia says. "It's part of our pre-performance routines and rituals. It's funny, we all made sure to empty our seventy-something bladders so we wouldn't wet ourselves on stage and we wind up barfing all over the place."

"We're nothing if not dignified," Jules says.

"So you all went to the restroom before going to the dressing room?" I ask.

They nod.

"Where and what did you see and who did you talk to?"

"I went to the little half-bath in the hallway under the stairs," Jules says. "It's the only bathroom directly between here and the stage. But someone was in it, so I ducked into my bathroom, did my business, and then went to the dressing room backstage. I remember seeing this young lady talking to my stepsons on the way to the bathroom and then in the kitchen on my way to the theater. I remember because she seemed in a bit of a panic."

I turn toward Carla.

"I did get in a little bit of a dither because Miss Dixie asked me to take over for her in the kitchen while she went to the restroom, but it was almost time for the toast and I needed to get over to the theater to get everything ready."

Jules says, "I also saw Max, Lavinia's . . . soon-to-be ex. He gave me a hangdog look and asked if he could talk to me. I figured he wanted to enlist my help with trying to get Lavinia not to divorce him and I wasn't having any part of that, so I told him I was late for the toast and they couldn't do it without me as I was the birthday girl, and I couldn't talk just then and to try me later in the night."

"Anyone else stand out?" I ask.

She shrugs. "I saw a lot of people during that time—well, all night, really. Oh, Tom and Randall wished me a happy birthday again, asked to meet with me again this week to try to reach some sort of settlement, and said they were sorry they couldn't stay for the performance."

"How about you two?" I ask, turning toward Nell and Lavinia.

"Saw a lot of people too," Lavinia says, "but didn't really get stopped by many since it wasn't my birthday."

"How long did y'all stay in here after Jules made her announcement and most of us started drifting toward the theater?" I ask.

They look at each other.

Nell shrugs. "Another five or ten minutes, maybe."

"Sounds about right," Lavinia says. "A little less maybe. Then I ducked into the little bathroom in the hallway."

"And I used the one in the theater," Nell says. "Well, actually, at first we both stood in line at the one in the hallway. Then we both had the idea to use the one in the theater—it's not private and it's out front not backstage, so we usually don't use it, but I really had to go, so . . ."

"Only design flaw of the entire house," Jules says. "I should've put another bathroom backstage."

"I told her to go ahead and use that one and I'd stay and use this one when it became available," Lavinia says.

"And who'd y'all talk to? What'd you see?"

"I didn't get to talk to him much," Nell says, "but I was very surprised to see Donnie Ray here."

"He better not have been here," Lavinia says. "And if he was . . . I better not find out you talked to him and didn't tell me."

"Lavinia," Nell says, "now wait just a—"

Cutting Nell off, Lavinia says, "Did anyone else see him?"

No one did.

Donnie Ray Bryant was Lilliana's father. He and Lillian had dated for a short while and he had become violent and began to stalk her once she broke things off with him. She had to get a restraining order against him and tried to have Lilliana without him knowing it. He's the reason Lavinia packs a small pistol.

"I told him he shouldn't be here," Nell says.

"Why didn't you tell me?" Lavinia says.

"I was going to, but then I got poisoned and almost died and accused of infecting you all with a virus I don't have, and it slipped my mind until now."

"You're sure he was here?" Lavinia says. "You didn't imagine it? Weren't on some of your essential herbs or something and—"

"He was here," she says. "I told him if you saw him you'd kill him and that he needed to go. He said not you nor anyone else was going to push him around anymore. I told him there were several cops here and he was going to get himself killed. He said he didn't care, but he left."

"Y'all said a lot not to have talked to him," Lavinia says. "Did Lillian see him?"

"She was already gone. I meant to tell you. Sorry I flaked. But I made sure he really left. It's why I was a little late getting to the dressing room."

"Where was this?" Jules asks. "Where did you see him?"

"On the back porch. I was on my way to the bathroom in the theater and saw him through the window, so stepped out there and told him to leave."

"I can't believe you didn't tell us," Lavinia says. "That's such a Nellie Bell thing to do."

"I'm sorry, Lavinia. I really am. If we hadn't been poisoned . . . I had every intention of telling you."

Lavinia turns toward me and Dad. "Can y'all go talk to him? Remind him what a restraining order is and see if you can get a sense of just how unhinged he is?"

Dad nods. "Of course."

"And please tell him for me that if he comes near me or my family again I will shoot the shit out of him."

"Tell him we all will," Jules says.

"Could he have been who poisoned us?" Lavinia asks.

"Certainly could be," I say. "We'll take a close look at him."

"Thank you."

"You okay to go on?" I ask.

She nods. "It's actually a lot less scary if it's someone like him. I'd expect something like that from someone like him. Creepy little . . ."

"Did y'all see or hear anything else that stands out to you?" I ask.

They both shake their heads.

"Do y'all mind if we go to the dressing room now?"

They indicate they don't, so we do.

On the way I tell Dixie that I'd like to talk to her when I finish in the theater, if she can hang around.

21

"I was the first one to arrive in here," Lavinia says.

We are in the small dressing room behind the stage. It has three stations, each with a countertop full of makeup, wigs, wax, latex, adhesives, and cleaners, a brightly lit mirror, and a thickly cushioned stool. Beside each stands a rack of costumes.

When we entered the room, each of the Queens sat at her makeup station as if on a throne.

Dad, Carla, and I are standing near and just outside the door. Ann went back to the farm to help Verna with the children.

"I was next," Nell says.

"And I was the caboose," Jules adds.

"But we all arrived within minutes of each other," Lavinia says.

The walls of the small room are covered with framed photos and posters from their performances over the years.

"Did anyone else come in?" I ask. "At any point?"

"A few people," Jules says. "Sayin' happy birthday and break a leg. I can't remember who all. And she came by to see if we needed anything." She nods towards Carla.

"Miss Dixie told me to duck my head in to see if they had everything they needed."

"And we did," Jules says.

"Then what?" I ask.

Jules says, "We changed into our costumes, freshened up our hair and makeup, did a few stretches and vocal warm-ups. Rehearsed our number. Had our circle. And went out on stage. Couldn't've been more normal."

"Had your circle?" I ask.

"Join hands," Lavinia says. "Ask God's blessings on our show."

"Or Goddess," Nell says.

"We've always done it," Jules says.

"Did you have anything to eat or drink back here?"

"Just our usual," Jules says. "But we didn't have anything in common—I mean none of us ate or drank out of the same thing or anything from the same source. Does that make sense?"

I nod. "What is 'the usual'?"

"For me," Lavinia says, "it's Throat Coat tea and honey."

"I have black tea and honey," Jules says.

Nell says, "I just have water and honey."

"So you all had honey," I say.

"We've always swallowed Tupelo honey before every performance," Jules says.

"Makes us sing sweeter," Nell says.

"It's very soothing to our throats," Lavinia says.

"And it goes with our name and who we are," Jules says. "But like the tea and water and anything else we have, we each have our own honey. It's all local, but it's not even from the same producers. We've never used the same bottles in case one of us has a sore throat or a cold or something."

"Or the 'rona," Lavinia says, glancing at Nell.

"I don't have the 'rona," she says.

"Who all knows your routine?" I ask.

They shrug.

"Everyone," Lavinia says.

"Anyone who's been around us before a show," Jules says. "It's no secret."

"Have you touched anything in here since Saturday night?" I ask.

"Haven't even been back in here," Jules says.

"Okay. Let's leave everything where it is in case we need to have any of it tested, and let's step over to the other dressing room."

22

A cross the back of the stage on the opposite side was a guest dressing room that was seldom used.

In it is a single makeup station surrounded by various set props, cleaning equipment, ladders and the like.

"This is where the champagne cart was, right?" I ask.

Jules nods. "Far as I know."

Carla nods. "It was in here."

"Did any of you come in here or see anyone coming or going before the show?" I ask.

They all shake their heads.

"Don't even remember glancing over in this direction," Nell says. "It's usually dark on this side."

"And it was Saturday night too," Carla says.

"Who all knew the champagne cart was in here?" I ask.

Jules shrugs. "Wasn't a secret. I'm sure Dixie and all her staff knew—and anyone who overheard us talking about it."

"We would've seen if someone came back here," Lavinia says. "Or someone would have seen them coming or going. No one was back here except for us."

"And her," Jules says, nodding toward Carla.

"And the people who stopped in to say happy birthday and break a leg."

"And whoever snuck in before any of us came over here," Nell says. "Not like any of this was locked. Anyone could've come back here during the first part of the party."

"That's a good point," Jules says. "We just have no way of knowing if anyone did or who did because anyone could have. The champagne sat over here a long time before anyone got here, so there was ample opportunity for someone to sneak in here and spike it."

"That's true," I say, "but it also wouldn't matter."

"Huh?" she says.

"Why the hell wouldn't it matter?" Lavinia asks.

"Because that wasn't the champagne y'all drank."

"Sure it is," Jules says.

"Actually, the bottle that was over here being chilled during the party wasn't the one you drank from. There was an accident."

Carla clears her throat and says, "I was rushing—running late getting over here, and I was nervous and it was dark and the bottle was slippery and . . . well, I dropped it. The bottle didn't break, but the cork popped when it hit the corner of the cart. So I freaked out. I rushed back over to the kitchen to ask Miss Dixie what to do. On the way, I remembered someone gave you a bottle of champagne for your birthday, so I dashed into the parlor and grabbed it. When I went into the kitchen to make sure that was okay with Miss Dixie, she wasn't there, so I just went with it. I brought it back here and put it in the ice so it could cool off some before the toast."

"Who gave you the bottle, Jules?" Lavinia asks.

"Tom and Randall," she says.

"So they were trying to kill you and because of an accident they nearly killed all of us."

"The little bastards," Jules says.

"Why haven't you arrested them?" Lavinia asks in what sounds more like a demand than a question.

"We've got an interview with them set up, but we've got to wait for the lab results to get back before we charge anyone. We're investigating them, though. Building a case."

"Could they really be so cold-blooded as to kill their step-mother over money?" Nell asks.

"It's a lot of money," Jules says.

23

———

"**I** think I may have been poisoned too," Dixie Ledoux is saying.

Carla, Dad, and I are back in the kitchen with her.

"Spent much of the night in the bathroom."

"Is that where you were when everyone was gathering in the theater?" I ask.

She shrugs. "Probably."

Though the same age as the Tupelo Queens, Dixie Ledoux looks older, and it's obvious she's had a much more difficult life. It shows in the deep worry and wrinkle lines etched into the pale, paper-thin skin of her perpetually scowling face, the guarded sadness and disappointment in her weary eyes, her stiff and bent body, and the way her extra weight has so unevenly misshapen it.

She is in no condition to be doing the work she is doing.

"So . . . not long before the Tupelo Queens make their way over to the theater," I say, "you asked Carla to fill in for you in the kitchen while you went to the bathroom, right?"

"While I went to the bathroom again," she says. "Yes. She happened to come in the kitchen when I had to go back to the bathroom, so I grabbed her. I wasn't even thinking that she was the one who had to roll the champagne cart out. Of course, I wasn't thinking I'd be in the bathroom that long either."

"Everything was fine," Carla says, "until I saw the Queens walk over, followed shortly by more and more of the crowd from over here. I was afraid they were going to call for the toast and turn to the wing waiting for the cart to be rolled out but nothing would happen."

"But fortunately I came out before that happened," Dixie says. "But just barely."

"That's when I rushed over and checked on the cart and everything . . . and dropped the bottle."

"You what?" Dixie asks.

Carla nods. "The bottle was slippery and it fell through my fingers."

"Did it break?"

"No, but . . ."

Carla explains again what happened and what she did.

"And," I say, "after she grabbed the gift bottle off the table in the parlor, she ran in here to ask you if that was okay, and you weren't here."

"I wasn't? Are you sure?"

Carla nods.

"But I told you to check to see if Jules and the others needed anything."

"That was the first time I went over," she says. "Before I broke the bottle."

Dixie looks at me. "I *did* have to go back to the bathroom again. I just didn't think it was that soon."

"Did you go anywhere else during that time?" I ask.

She shakes her head.

"Did you go watch the show and join in the toast?"

She shakes her head. "Wouldn't have anyway. Too much to

do over here—all the cleaning and what not—but with how I was feeling . . . I never ventured that far from the bathroom."

"Do you really believe you were poisoned?" Dad asks.

She shrugs. "Never been so sick in all my life. You can't imagine how it was coming out of both ends of me."

And I don't want to—not of anyone, but especially the person preparing the food for the party.

"How much contact with the Queens did you have?" Dad asks. "Did you eat or drink anything in common with them?"

"Mostly just Jules. It was her party. She's who hired me. But I seen all of 'em at different times. And I didn't have any caviar or champagne if that's what you mean."

"They had caviar that night?" Dad asks.

"Just meant I can't keep up with their extravagances and indulgences. I'm the hired help. Don't have anything in common with them, including diet."

"Y'all have high school in common," Dad says.

"Going to the same high school don't mean you had a common experience. They's different even back then. Always have been."

"In what way?"

"It's like they always been queens and the rest of us just their humble servants."

"Sounds like you resent them," Dad says.

"Yeah, and that's why after seventy years I decided to kill them," she says. "Finally reached my limit. I will tell you this . . . Nobody, and I mean nobody—not even the sheriff and brother of one of the victims—better say that they got food poisoning from my food. 'Cause I *will* have to kill somebody then."

24

"He was there?" Lillian says. "Really?"

"According to Nell."

On the way home, I take a detour into Pine County to check on Lillian Pritchett and to see if she has seen or heard from Donnie Ray.

Though she assures me it's not necessary, I remain outside and over six feet away from her. She's standing in her doorway and I'm in the front yard.

"There are more reliable witnesses," she says. "Did anyone else see him?"

"Haven't really asked around yet," I say. "We plan to. I just wanted to make sure you were okay and to let you know what Nell said."

"I'm so glad I left early," she says. "I felt so guilty, but if he was really there, maybe my grief saved me from—I was gonna say *something worse*, but I'm not sure there is anything."

I nod and frown. "I'm so sorry."

We are quiet for a few moments as silent tears stream down her face.

"You wouldn't think I could be this upset for this long over someone I knew for a matter of weeks, but . . . I've never felt so connected with anyone in my life—and that started while she was still growing inside me."

"I understand that completely. I feel the same way about mine."

"So I'm not crazy?"

"Of course not," I say. "You know that."

"Sometimes I don't. I can tell people are ready for me to quit being so sad all the time. A lot of people have just stopped coming around—and long before the pandemic."

"That's . . . They just don't know what to say, how to help. It's on them, not you. But you've got to feel so lonely, so isolated—and on top of dealing with all the grief. Anna I would love to have you over anytime. I hope you know that."

"I do. Thank you. I've joined an online grief support group. It's weird and awkward to do it via video chat, but . . . it's not terrible and may even be beneficial."

We talk about her grieving process some more, and I try to be as supportive and helpful as I can be, though I'm not sure I do her any good.

Eventually, our conversation returns to Donnie Ray Bryant.

"Nell is a little nuts," she says. "I love her like a crazy old hippie aunt, but . . . I wouldn't be surprised to find out he really wasn't there at all."

"I'll try to get confirmation either way," I say. "So he hasn't harassed you in any way since the restraining order?"

"I haven't heard a peep out of him," she says. "If he's still stalking me, he's doing it in stealth mode. And that sort of defeats the purpose, doesn't it?"

"Yeah, sort of does."

"Do you think he could be behind the poisoning some-how?" she asks. "Could he have been trying to kill me or me and Grandma—or just random friends of ours?"

"It's something we're going to look into," I say. "Just be on your guard and let me know if you see or hear or feel anything at all that might be him."

She nods. "This'll be a good test of my will to live," she says. "Hard to want to most of the time. Grandma bought me a gun, but I'm not sure I could use it even if he broke in and was trying to kill me. I'm really not."

"Would you like to come ride out the quarantine with us?" I ask. "We'd love to have you."

"That's so kind of you. Grandma keeps trying to get me to move in with her—and I might now that Max is moving out. But the truth is I really do prefer to be alone."

TUESDAY, MARCH 24, 2020

Tuesday, March 24, 2020
65,800 confirmed cases and 681 deaths in the US

The Tokyo Olympics are delayed until 2021.

"I would love to have the country opened up and just raring to go by Easter," President Trump says at a Fox News town hall. "I think Easter Sunday—you'll have packed churches all over our country. There is tremendous hope as we look forward and we begin to see the light at the end of the tunnel."

25

"My clients weren't even there when it happened," Rigby La Fontaine is saying.

He's a trim, charming, polished forty-something man in an expensive suit and even more expensive Italian shoes, and is Tom and Randall Foster's attorney.

"I appreciate your need to investigate and I sympathize that you have so little you're grasping for straws here," he continues, "but my clients have nothing germane to add. They weren't even there."

Dad and Gerald Woodson are in the Potter County Sheriff's Department interview room with La Fontaine, Tom, and Randall. I'm in the dim A/V room observing on the monitor as the interview is being recorded.

Each of the men in the interview room are at least six feet from one another. Tom and Randall are wearing the elusive N-95 masks, which quickly sold out across the country and are now impossible to find. Their attorney and the two law enforcement officers interviewing them aren't wearing masks of any kind.

"You know as well as I do," Woodson says, "you don't have

to be present when someone is poisoned to have poisoned them, but that's beside the point. The point is—"

"*Whoa*, hold up just a minute there, partner," La Fontaine says. "Are you actually accusing my clients of having something to do with the alleged poisoning?"

"No, sir, I'm not."

"Because I was told you were interested in interviewing them as potential witnesses, not suspects."

"We are," Woodson says. "They aren't suspects yet. They are potential wit—"

"*Yet?*" La Fontaine says, his voicing rising in pitch and volume.

"I didn't mean—"

"If you've got us here for some sort of fishing expedition so you can trump up some false charges against them, I'd be derelict in my duty as an officer of the court to let them sit here another second."

"It's nothing like that."

"It sounds exactly like that."

"If you'll just let me—"

"I understand the sheriff here was at the party and is actually related to the victim," La Fontaine says. "Has he been interviewed like this? Is he a suspect?"

"I have and I am," Dad says. "Everyone there that night is a person of interest—and will remain so until we know more."

"That's fine," La Fontaine says, "but what about all the other people on the planet who weren't there? Investigator Woodson just pointed out that one need not be present when someone is poisoned to have been the poisoner."

Woodson starts to say something, but La Fontaine interrupts him.

"Gentlemen, these are dangerous times," he says. "It's not only irresponsible of you to be conducting interviews right now, but it's irresponsible of me to even let my clients be here.

But they insisted because they are innocent and have nothing to hide and had hoped all this could be cleared up quickly and painlessly—but that doesn't seem to be the case, so I'm inclined to halt this little witch hunt right here."

"All the theatrics and histrionics aren't necessary," Dad says. "We just have a few questions. You mentioned me being related to one of the victims. So are your clients. I would think they'd want to help us catch whoever tried to kill their stepmother."

"That crazy bitch was never our stepmother."

Because of the masks I can't tell if Tom or Randall had been the one to say it.

"Okay, we're done here," La Fontaine says, standing. "Come on guys. Time for us to go."

The Fosters stand and the three men storm out of the room without another word.

"That went well," Dad says.

"Coulda been worse," Woodson says.

"I believe the phrase you're looking for is *coulda been better*," Dad says. "Hard to imagine it bein' any worse. He just handed you your ass without even breaking a sweat, so . . . yeah, not sure it *coulda been worse*."

THURSDAY, MARCH 26, 2020

Thursday, March 26, 2020
81,321 confirmed cases and 1,159 deaths in the US

The United States officially becomes the country hardest hit by the pandemic, with at least 81,321 confirmed infections and more than a thousand deaths.

26

———

On the day that our country officially becomes the number one epicenter for the COVID-19 global pandemic crisis, we find out the results of our tests.

"Your test came back negative," Zaire says. "Sorry for the delay. I really underestimated the backlog for the lab I used."

Anna and I are in the kitchen talking and preparing dinner, the girls are in their room playing.

"What about the others?" I ask.

"I can only tell you your results," she says. "You'll have to ask the others about theirs."

"Have you already notified them?" I ask.

"I have two more to do. Is Anna there with you?"

"Here she is, and thank you again," I say, passing Anna my phone.

When Anna ends the call, she hands me the phone and returns to cooking without saying a word.

"Well?" I say.

"Well what?"

"What'd she say?"

She shakes her head. "Can't," she says. "HIPPA. But you

already know. Much air as we share . . . Got to be the same as yours."

"Wonder if anyone tested positive," I say. "Most curious about Nell."

"If you wait another minute or two, you can call Jules and find out everyone's results. I'm sure they're all talking and texting away about it right now."

"I'm sure you're—"

My phone begins vibrating again. We both laugh when we see who it is.

I leave the phone on the counter and press Speaker.

"Hey, Aunt Jules," I say.

"If you and your lovely wife are negative then we all are," she says.

"Then we all are."

"Thanks be," she says. "I was worried about poor Nellie Bell, but not even she has it. It's such a relief. I'd rather die of poisoning than that wicked shit."

"Let's just make sure you don't die of either."

"I second that emotion," she says. "Any other developments?"

"Your stepsons weren't helpful," I say.

"Jack told me," she says. "Said they had a real laidback and reasonable lawyer too."

"Yeah, he was a real sweetheart."

"I hope it was them," she says. "It'd mean Nell and Lavinia are safe."

"Soon as we get the tox tests back, we'll go at them again."

"It's made me feel better about Nell going forward with her party."

"She's really saying she is?"

"Seems determined," she says. "Quarantine isn't much being followed or enforced around here so . . . She plans to do a very, very small gathering in her backyard with social distancing and no touching. Says she's never missed one yet and isn't about to start now. Lavinia says she's not going and it's not because of the virus. Told Nell she should do a 'lambs to the slaughter' theme."

"I rarely agree with Lavinia on anything," I say, "but . . . she's being the reasonable one for once."

"Maybe it really is the end of the world," she says.

"You're not gonna go, are you?"

"I have to. Especially since Lavinia isn't. Can't leave poor ol' Nellie Bell by herself. Don't get me wrong. I don't want to die. But it won't be long until I do—no matter how careful or cautious I am. There are worse things than going out with a lifelong friend at her birthday party. A lot worse things."

SUNDAY, MARCH 29, 2020

Sunday, March 29, 2020
161,800 confirmed cases and 2,431 deaths in the US

The US death toll rises over two thousand, doubling in just two days.

"The better you do, the faster this whole nightmare will end," President Trump says at a White House Rose Garden press conference. "Therefore, we will be extending our guidelines to April 30th to slow the spread. We can expect that, by June 1st, we will be well on our way to recovery. We think, by June 1st, a lot of great things will be happening."

27

———

"They can gather at the grocery store," Willie Baker is saying, "but not at the house of God. Woe unto those who would feed the belly but not the soul."

He is behind his pulpit preaching in direct disobedience to the shelter-in-place order given by Mayor Ronald Long.

A handful of people are spread out in the pews of the small AME church, amen-ing his every sentiment.

Dad and I are standing in the back, waiting for Potter County deputies to arrive. Dad asked me to come along to talk to Willie if he resisted.

"They can gather at the hospitals and clinics, but not at the house of God," he continues.

"All right now," one of the congregants says. "Preach it."

"Woe unto the nation that submits to the medicines of man," Baker says, "but neglects the Great Physician, by whose stripes we are healed, who offers us total and complete healing."

"Complete healing," one of his church members echoes.

When the two white deputies arrive, they are wearing riot gear, one carrying a shotgun, the other a rifle.

Dad directs them right back out the door they came in.

"The hell is this?" he says, out in front of the little church. "Get that shit off right now."

As they begin to take off the body armor, he turns to me. "See why I wanted to be the one to do this and have you here?"

Turning back to the two, who had removed everything but their helmets and still held their riot weapons, Dad says, "What were you thinking?"

"That there might be trouble," the taller, slightly older of the two men says.

"From seven unarmed old people at church?"

"The preacher's an ex-con," the shorter, stouter deputy says.

From where she sits in her car, a middle-aged woman wearing a bandana for a mask is filming us.

"I realize this is a difficult job," Dad says. "But we can very easily make it much harder than it has to be. You two come to my office in the morning and let's discuss appropriate and reasonable responses and talk about some additional training I want our department to do. Now, put all your riot gear, including your weapons, in your trunk, and let's get back in there and see if we can't enforce the law peaceably."

We walk back into the small church a few moments later.

"There's a balm in Gilead," Baker is saying, "an everlasting fountain flowing from the wound in the spear-pierced side of our Lord Jesus Christ. No virus that's ever been or ever will be is equal to the blood of Jesus."

"No virus," someone in the congregation says.

Dad walks down the aisle and says, "Folks, I'm real sorry to have to do this, but the mayor has issued a shelter-at-home order and I'm afraid we have to enforce it. Please leave peaceably. Go home and stay there. This is all temporary. Just until we flatten the curve of the spread of this awful virus. You'll be back here worshiping together in no time."

"Be strong in Jesus's name," Baker says.

"Anyone who won't leave on their own will be arrested," Dad says. "And that's something we don't want to do."

"We obey the laws of God, not the laws of man," Baker says.

"There's no law of God that says you have to be here right now," Dad says. "Please be reasonable."

"Forsake not the assembling of yourselves together," Baker says. "Where two or more are gathered together in my name, there am I in the midst of them."

Dad turns toward Baker. "Will you not do what's right for yourself and your congregation and leave on your own?"

"I will not leave this watchtower the Lord has posted me on," Baker says. "No, sir, I will not."

"Then you're under arrest," Dad says.

The two deputies now in masks, face shields, and gloves but without any riot gear, approach Baker as he continues to preach.

When they reach him, he puts his hands behind his back to be cuffed without ever missing a beat.

As Dad had hoped, when Baker is led out, the others follow.

"Strike down the shepherd and the sheep will be scattered," Baker says as he sees the others getting into their cars.

"We'll be prayin' for you, Brother Willie," someone yells from an open car window as they drive away.

"God bless you and keep you," someone else says.

"I'm sorry about this," Dad says. "This isn't something I ever wanted to do, but you gave me no choice. I have to enforce the laws. I'm sworn to do so. And it's for your own good—and that of your congregation. But the truth is . . . you'd be far more at risk of being exposed to the virus in the county jail than you were just then in your little church, so . . . I'm gonna have my men take you home instead of jail, but please don't make us have to do this again. If we have to do it again, we will take you to jail. We'll have to."

28

———

Things don't go as well at Leviticus Lanier's Pentecostal church across town.

With the other two deputies taking Willie Baker home, two different deputies meet us at Joyful Noise Holiness Pentecostal Tabernacle.

Unlike the two that met us at the AME church, they aren't wearing any riot gear, and I wonder if it shows a difference in the deputies or a difference in how they approach a white versus a black congregation.

After explaining to them why we're here, what the objectives are, and how to best go about achieving them, Dad gives them a few important reminders and we walk inside.

The building is larger and has more members than Willie Baker's church, but most of the pews are empty and the people are spread out—though not in any discernible pattern related to social distancing.

When we reach about the halfway mark of the center aisle, four middle-aged men with weapons—two in front of us and two behind us—step out to block the aisle. Each has on black slacks, a black tie, and black shoes. A badge identifying them as security is pinned to the pockets of their white shirts.

Though the shotguns and rifles they carry are out and at the ready, they remain pointed at the ground.

We stop walking, Dad and one deputy facing forward, me and the other deputy turning to face the back.

Leviticus Lanier stops preaching mid-sentence, an insipid grin spreading across his face.

Looking directly at us, he says, "Law of man, meet the rod of God. We're not going to sit here like lambs to the slaughter while someone comes in and shoots us—be he Muslim terrorist, demon-possessed lunatic, or misguided lawman."

Ignoring Lanier, Dad addresses the men in front of him loud enough for everyone to hear.

"We are duly appointed law enforcement officers here to peaceably enforce the mayor and governor's lawful order not to congregate during this global health crisis. It's for your own good. And it will be obeyed. Now, I have not drawn my weapon. Neither have the law enforcement officers with me. And we don't want to. But know this—we are trained professionals. We will not stand here and let you point or fire those weapons at us. If you attempt to shoot us, we will return fire, and no matter how much time you've spent training for this moment, we've spent decades more. You will not only be shot but you will be arrested. And you will spend most of the rest of your life in prison for shooting at a law enforcement officer. Leviticus will get some headlines and a little publicity, but you will be in custody or in the ground. This is the single most important decision of your life up until this moment. Make the right one. Place your weapons on the floor and back away from them. You get one chance."

Leviticus starts to say something, but Dad cuts him off.

"Everyone in here listen to me," he says, even louder. "This is a temporary order for your own protection and that of your neighbors. No one is trying to stop you from worshiping. We're just not allowed to gather in groups right now. It won't last long, but—"

"Are you going to obey God?" Leviticus says. "Or man?"

I say very loudly since I'm facing the back, "Jesus said 'render unto Caesar what is Caesar's.' He said 'do unto others as you would have them do unto you.' We can carry the virus and not know it. We can feel just fine and unintentionally give it an older person or a compromised person and actually kill them without meaning to. What would Jesus do? He'd take care of the sick and weak and wounded. He'd make sure to do his part to protect them. He'd obey a reasonable, temporary order that is only meant to protect vulnerable people. And he would worship in spirit and truth from his home. And, in fact, when you stay home and worship with your family, he will be with you. 'For where two or three gather in my name, there am I with them.'"

As if nothing out of the ordinary is happening, Leviticus returns to his sermon, preaching to an increasingly disinterested congregation.

The four men place their weapons on the floor—first one, then the other three following closely behind—as one by one the congregants begin to gather their Bibles and ease down the aisle and out of the sanctuary.

As the deputies move to secure the weapons, I scan the pews, and Dad steps to the front and onto the platform, and places Leviticus, who continues to preach, under arrest.

29

I'm surprised when Paul Branch opens the door at Jasmine Carter's house. The last I had heard she had kicked him out after he got physical with Nash.

He seems surprised by me too—but more by my mask than my presence here.

"Is this a stickup?" he asks, holding his hands up. "You here to rob us?"

I lift the guitar case slightly. "Stopped by to drop this off for Nash. He around?"

"Where else would he be?" he says. "He's here all the goddamn time. Whole world's locked down. No school. No stores. No church. Nowhere to go. And now not only will he be here all the time, but he'll be making racket on that thing, so thanks for that."

He yells for Nash, but it's Jasmine who appears behind him.

"Hey, John," she says. "Come on in. Paul, where are your manners?"

"Don't want to the run this risk of infecting you guys," I say. "Shouldn't have anyone in your home right now, but especially someone like me. I'm still around a lot of people, and though I try to wear a mask and practice social distancing, all essential workers are extremely high risk."

"Don't be silly," she says. "Come on in."

"Thank you, but I can't."

"We all tested negative," she says. "You did too. Besides, we're very healthy people. We don't meet—"

"I do," Paul says.

"I mean me and the boys," she says. "A good diet of healthy, fresh, non-processed food is the key. Not synthetic medicines, insane inoculations, and expensive supplements—weak powered versions of things that you should be getting in your diet anyway. I'm not sayin' I'm completely against medicine like my mom. Paul convinced me to take antidepressants, and they've made a world of difference for me. But don't tell Mom. She wouldn't understand. Hell, she never even took me to the doctor. I had to ask your aunt and Lavinia who to go to. Sorry for going on and on. Anyway, I was just making fresh fruit smoothies. Would you like one?"

"Thank you, but I really can't. And I need to go. Is Nash around? I'd like to see him for a minute before I do."

"Sure, let me get him."

They drift back into the house, leaving the door open.

I step back down the walkway several feet, set the guitar case down, and then move about eight feet beyond it.

When Nash finally comes outside, Jasmine is with him.

Glancing over her shoulder and lowering her voice she says, "He's having a hard time with Paul being back."

"I was surprised that he was," I say.

"We had a good long talk," she says. "He's going to leave all the parenting of Nash up to me, so we won't have any more . . . incidents like before. Anyway, could you talk to him?"

"Paul?" I ask, though I know what she means.

"What? No. Nash."

I nod and she rushes back in the house, closing the door behind her this time.

"Here's the guitar I promised you," I say. "Sorry it took me longer to bring it by than I thought it would."

"Thanks," he says.

He kneels down and opens the case, revealing the Epiphone Masterbilt acoustic guitar with the violin burst finish inside.

"Cool," he says. "This is a nice one."

"Hope you enjoy it," I say. "I want front row seats at your first concert."

He sits on the walkway, pulls the guitar from the case, and begins to noodle around with it.

"Sounds good, man," I say.

"Thanks."

I can tell he's excited to have the guitar, but there's an underlying sadness that prevents him from enjoying anything thoroughly.

"I'm sorry your mom let Paul move back in," I say.

He frowns and shakes his head. "She's so dumb. He's a . . . loudmouth idiot and a . . ."

"Bully?" I offer.

"Yeah, I guess. He's just so fake and . . . he stands for and does everything she says she's against, but she still takes him back over and over and does what he tells her to. It's like she can't be alone. Can't make her own decisions."

"I know things are difficult now," I say. "I know you're frustrated and feel like you don't have a lot of say over your own life, but . . . You get to decide what kind of person you want to be. You get to shape who you become. You're smart. You're strong. You're resourceful. You're talented. And most of all you're kind. You get to decide what kind of person you're going to be now and what kind of man you'll be when you're grown and have a place of your own. Your mom can't decide that for you. Neither can Paul. Only you. And it can be helpful to know what you don't want to be like as well as knowing what you do want to be like."

"Don't want to be like them," he says.

"Then don't be," I say. "Decide not to, then take the steps necessary not to be. It will take some work, but you can do it, and I can help you."

"Whatever I have to do," he says. "Just let me know."

"Cool," I say. "We can talk about it more over time and I'll give you a few books to read."

Because of the quarantine and social distancing I hadn't intended to have him over, but I'm finding it difficult not to take him away, however temporarily, from the situation he's in.

"The virus is very dangerous," I say. "But only for some people. Older people like my dad and your grandmother. Sick and compromised people. We've all got to do our part for them. Staying in and social distancing is to save them."

He nods.

"So that means we have to stay at least six feet away from each other," I say.

"I don't mind," he says.

"If you don't mind doing that from us and us doing that from you," I say, "then I'd love to have you come over and stay with us tonight—have dinner, play the guitar, hang out, maybe watch a movie."

He quickly but carefully places the guitar in the case and latches it. "Let me tell Mom."

"Ask her," I say. "Don't tell her."

"That's what I meant, but she won't mind. And he'll be happy to have me gone."

"Then he's a bigger loser than I thought," I say, "and his loss is our gain."

FRIDAY, APRIL 3, 2020

Friday, April 3, 2020
273,880 confirmed cases and 7,006 deaths in the US

The global pandemic has sickened more than one million people in 171 countries across six continents, killing at least fifty-one thousand.

Nearly ten million Americans are out of work, including a staggering 6.6 million people who applied for unemployment benefits during the last week of March. The speed and scale of the job losses is without precedent. Before this, the worst week for unemployment filings was 695,000 in 1982.

"But it's not the flu," President Trump says at a White House Coronavirus Task Force briefing. "It's vicious. When you send a friend to the hospital and you call up to find out, how is he doing, it happened to me. Where he goes to the hospital, he says goodbye, sort of a tough guy, little older, little heavier than he'd like to be, frankly. And you call up the next day, 'How's he doing?' And he's in a coma? This is not the flu. But I said it was going away—and it is going away."

30

"Toxicology results are back," I say.

Anna and I are on a Zoom videoconference meeting with Jules, Lavinia, Nell, Carla, Jasmine, Lillian, Dixie, Merrill, Zaire, Dad, and Gerald Woodson.

Because of the COVID-19 quarantine, more and more business, families, and friend groups are connecting via Zoom, Skype, and other videoconferencing platforms.

Though I'm on the call ostensibly as a witness like everyone else who as at the party, and my involvement in the investigation is unofficial, Gerald's expression and demeanor make it clear he's not happy about it. He has his mic muted, and I'll be surprised if he utters a single word during the conversation.

"*And*?" Jules asks.

"The lab found no traces of oxycodone or any other poison in the champagne bottle or the glasses."

"What?" she says. "But—"

"So I didn't poison anybody," Carla says. "I mean . . . by grabbing the . . . by dropping the first bottle and grabbing the other . . . I didn't . . . That's not what caused the . . ."

"So Tom and Randall didn't try to kill me," Jules says.

I shrug. "Just because it wasn't in the bottle they brought you doesn't mean they weren't behind it," I say. "Would've been a little on the nose to put it in their gift."

"I guess so."

"I'm confused," Nell says. "What does—"

"So how *did* we get poisoned then?" Lavinia asks.

The audio and video quality of each person in our Zoom differs greatly depending on the device and equipment they have and the internet speed of the provider they're using. Carla and Nell's are by far the worst.

"When I read about how oxycodone works," I say, "I began to doubt that it was in the champagne—not just because of the difficulty or impossibility of getting it in the bottle but because none of you reported the champagne smelling or tasting any differently. Oxy is bitter. You would've noticed it. It also takes about twenty to thirty minutes to work, so . . . it couldn't have been the champagne unless it was a different type of poison— one that works immediately. It only appeared to be the champagne because it started working so soon after y'all drank it. But from the moment y'all told me you all took honey before your performance, I began to suspect that may have been how you were poisoned. Not only was the timing right but the sweetness of the honey would have helped cover the bitterness of the oxy. After meeting with you in your dressing room, I took samples of the honey and called Russell Walters, the crime scene investigator at FDLE who processed the scene, and let him know what I was thinking and asked if I could send him the samples to test. He called me an idiot and said he was offended that I would think for one second that he hadn't gathered and tested samples of everything in your dressing room from that night—the tea, water, honey, etc. Anyway, he tested nearly everything in the house—including several items from the kitchen, both food and drink. And the only substance to come back positive for oxy was the honey."

"So the Tupelo Queens were poisoned with Tupelo honey," Anna says. "That's got to be significant."

I nod. "Hard to see how it wouldn't be."

"So," Jules says, "it's far more personal and was definitely meant for all of us—not just me with these two being collateral damage."

"Certainly what it appears to be," I say. "Of course, that could be a cover. It could have been made to look that way to conceal the real motive, but it seems to be personal, specific, and directed toward all three of you."

"Who could hate all three of us that much?" Lavinia says. "I couldn't even see how each of us could have someone that hates us that much, but for one person to hate all three of us that much . . ."

Everyone is quiet for a moment, letting Lavinia's chilling words wash over us.

"Can anyone think of someone who would want all three of you dead?" I ask.

After a long few moments of thinking, no one is able to come up with anything.

"So we're no closer to finding out who tried to kill us now than we were when it happened," Lavinia says. "And we're all equally in danger."

Jules says, "We probably all need to be more cautious."

"Unless the murderer is the UPS man," Nell says, "or the Amazon employee who ships my packages, I think I'm good. Never see anyone else."

"I don't think you're taking this seriously enough," Lavinia says. "And while we're on the subject, I think you should cancel your birthday."

"Well, I'm not going to, so save your breath."

Jules says, "She doesn't mean cancel. She means postpone."

"As if the pandemic isn't reason enough," Lavinia says, "the poisoner definitely tips the scales toward postponement."

"I'll take every precaution and I'll keep the guest list small, but I'm not about to cancel. You don't have to come if you don't want to."

"I want to come, but I just can't," Lavinia says. "Please postpone it. I really don't want to miss it, but I have a heartbroken granddaughter to think about. We wouldn't just be risking ourselves but all those who depend on us. And it's doubly risky now. There's a virus and a person trying to kill us."

"I understand all that," Nell says. "And I won't blame anyone who doesn't come, but I'm not postponing it. Besides, I think it might be our best chance of catching the bastard. John, when we get finished can you call me to talk about an idea I have for how to catch him?"

"Or *her*," Lavinia says, "and getting back to that—" she looks from Dad to me and back again "—y'all are starting over again at square one, aren't you? If it wasn't the Foster boys' champagne . . . It could be anybody, right? Anyone could've snuck in and poisoned each of our honey bottles at any time during the night, right?"

"Actually," Jules says, "the theater was locked during most of the party. Well, at least more than half of it."

"Who all has a key?" Dad asks. "When was it unlocked and who unlocked it?"

"The answer to all three is the same," she says. "*Me*. I'm the only one with a key. At some point I went over to check the temperature to make sure it was cool enough—or would be once we all got over there breathing and moving around."

"And when was that?"

"Let's see . . ." she says, looking up and squinting as she twists her lips back and forth. "Not too long before I went into the den to tell the girls it was almost time to head over."

"How long before?" I say. "It's important."

She shakes her head and shrugs. "I can't be positive. Maybe ten minutes before. No more than twenty."

"That really narrows down the window of opportunity," I say. "When you came back over, was anyone lingering in the hallway or near the theater door? Or did you see anyone go inside?"

She shakes her head. "Sorry. No one."

"And Nell, you were the first to arrive in the theater, right?" I say.

"I think I was."

"The first out of you three or the very first period?"

"I'm pretty sure I was the very first," she says.

"Did you see anyone? Do you remember who came in next?"

"I didn't see anyone," she says. "Not when I walked to the back to use the restroom—and by the way, I went to the dressing room first. I wasn't paying much attention . . . my mind was somewhere else—as usual. Anyway, I walked into the theater, then backstage to the dressing room, then remembered I needed to wee before we sang, so then walked back out, across the stage, through the theater, and into the bathroom in the back. I said all that to say that I think I was the first one in the theater and I think I would've seen if anyone else was anywhere in there."

"Could the honey have been poisoned at a different time?" I ask. "Earlier in the day or the week?"

Jules shakes her head. "Our dressing room door always stays locked—even when the theater is unlocked. We rehearsed the day before and all took our water, tea, and honey—so it was fine then—and the dressing room remained locked from then until I unlocked it when I unlocked the theater about fifteen or twenty minutes before we all went over."

"So," Dad says, "the poison had to be introduced into the honey sometime in the half hour or so between you unlocking the theater and y'all taking it."

31

"We really need to pinpoint everyone's movements during that narrow window of opportunity," Dad says. "Why don't we start with all of us on this call—and not just our movements but who we saw, then we'll branch out from there."

Dixie says, "I never left the kitchen except to go to the restroom, which was less than twenty feet away."

Carla's expression seems to contradict that, but she doesn't say anything. I'll have to ask her about it in private.

The Queens reiterate what they had told us previously. Jules went to the kitchen to check in after unlocking the theater, then went around announcing that it was almost time for the toast. After leaving the den, she used the restroom in her bedroom, then made her way to the theater, getting stopped along the way by friends and family.

"Did you see or speak to anyone coming from the theater?" I ask.

"Max," she says. "He asked if I had seen Lavinia. I pointed him in the direction of the den or the bathroom."

"*My* Max?" Lavinia says.

Jules nods.

"I'm sorry to ask this so bluntly," I say, "but if something happens to you while you're still married . . ."

"He gets the house and about a quarter of my money," she says. "But he wouldn't hurt me—or anyone—for anything, and certainly not for money."

"If something happens to you after you two divorce," I say.

"He gets nothing. Of course."

"And you've told him you want a divorce?" I say.

"Yes, but I'm telling you, he wouldn't kill anyone. I'm certain of that."

"One hundred percent," Lillian says. "I agree with Grandma completely. Max wouldn't kill anyone."

"Who gets the other three-quarters of your estate?" I ask.

"My granddaughter, Lillian," she says. "But she also wouldn't do anything to hurt me. I'm even more certain of that than I am of Max—and I'm absolutely certain of Max. I give her whatever she wants now."

"She does," Lillian says. "I'd rather have her around than all the money in the world. Have everything I want except the one thing I can't have."

I nod. "I'm sorry. And I'm sorry for all the questions, but they all have to be asked."

"Completely understand," she says.

"Plus," Lavinia says, "following your reasoning . . . if she was trying to kill me, which she is not, wouldn't she wait until she would get everything and not just three-quarters of it?"

Jules says, "It also looked like Sue Ann Gibson was coming from the theater, but I didn't speak to her."

"Why was she even there?" Nell asks. "I know you didn't invite her."

"She crashed," Jules says. "No other explanation. What needs an explanation is why. She didn't say anything to you? Figured whatever she was doing here had to do with you."

"Yeah," Lavinia says, "like tryin' to get you to take Carson's sorry ass back."

"Or poison me for lettin' her have him in the first place," Nell says. "She didn't say boo to me."

"Where were Tom and Randall when they told you they weren't staying for the performance?" I ask.

"Had to be close to the theater doors," she says, "because I saw them after I saw Max. Didn't seem to be coming from the theater, but . . . doesn't mean they weren't."

"Their motive is far greater than Max's," Lavinia says. "I'm not worth anything close to what Jules is."

"I've just told y'all what I did," Nell says. "And Donnie Ray is about the only person I talked to."

"Still can't believe he was there," Lillian says.

"He could've easily been there to hurt us," Lavinia says. "I'm just glad you had already left."

"Me too, Grandma. Something was guiding me to go, taking care of me."

"Careful talking like that," Nell says. "She'll kick you out of the family."

"We believe in the guidance of God and guardian angels," Lavinia says. "Just not a bunch of rocks and tea leaves and dime store tarot cards."

Jasmine says, "I'm glad to hear you talk like that, Lilly. It'll help you heal. Just stay open."

"I'm trying," Lillian says, her voice restraining some frustration and condescension beneath.

Lavinia says, "Jack, have y'all talked to Donnie Ray yet?"

"Still trying to locate him," Dad says, "but we will. And I've got deputies patrolling Lillian's home and neighborhood."

"Good," she says. "The sooner the better."

"Lillian," I say, "I know you left early, but did you see or hear anything suspicious?"

"Sorry," she says. "I'm afraid I'm not gonna be any help at all."

"That's okay," I say.

"I'm not sure if you're going in any kind of order," Jasmine says, "but I'll just go ahead and let you know the only people I was surprised to see were Mom's ex and his new wife. Never observed them acting suspicious, but just their being there was suspicious, you know?"

Nell says, "Sue Ann was there, but not Carson."

"No, I saw them both," Jasmine says. "It's odd. I never saw them together, but they were both there."

"I assume you'll be talking to both of them," Nell says.

"Absolutely," Dad says.

"And my movements were similar to Jules's and Nell's," Jasmine says, "—except I went to the bathroom in the house and I didn't really talk to anyone."

Carla says, "As y'all know, I was in a tizzy—running around everywhere, holding down the fort for Miss Dixie until she returned from the bathroom. Then I rushed backstage, broke the champagne, then ran back into the house and grabbed another bottle. I feel like I saw everybody and nobody."

"And you don't remember seeing anyone backstage?" I ask. "Or headed away from or toward it?"

She shrugs. "I may have, but if I did, I just don't remember. Sorry."

Merrill says, "We been concentrating on the theater, but what about Jules's bathroom? Mama said she saw Graham Arnold come from back there that night."

It's a great question.

Often referred to as "the Mayor," Graham Arnold is a middle-aged man with mental and emotional issues who spends most of his time walking Main Street, waving and speaking to the citizens of Pottersville—when he's not too busy talking to himself. It seems as if every small Southern town has someone like the Mayor, who the entire town helps take care of. Someone usually makes sure he gets to and from most of the gatherings in the area, where he not only fills his stomach but his pockets with whatever is on offer.

Jasmine says, "Didn't he poison his mama or somebody when he was younger?"

"His aunt who raised him," Dad says. "But it was ruled an accident. The investigators and the state's attorney's office agreed he didn't know what he was doing, so no charges were ever filed. But we'll definitely still talk to him."

Merrill says, "Anybody else see anyone going into or coming out of Jules's bedroom or bathroom?"

"I saw a few people emerging from back there throughout the night," Lavinia says. "Didn't stand out. Thought they were just using the restroom for overflow."

"Same here," Nell says.

"Probably had to because of how I was bogarting the other bathroom most of the night," Dixie says.

"Didn't think anything of it at the time," Carla says, "but I saw at least one of Jules's stepsons come out of there, but I couldn't tell you which one—and I may have seen them both at different times. Full disclosure—I went in the bedroom one time. More for a breather than anything else but I did use the bathroom too."

"I did too," Lillian says.

"I bet most of us did," Jasmine says. "Was always a line at the other one."

Carla says, "I also saw Max, Sue Ann, Graham, and Paul at different times throughout the night. I'll let you know as others come to me—if they do."

"Paul who?" Jasmine asks.

"Your Paul," she says. "Branch."

"He didn't come with us," Jasmine says. "We were split up at the time. He wasn't there."

"He may not have been there long," Carla says, "but he was there. I saw him."

"Must've been someone who looked like him," Jasmine says. "He wasn't even in town that night."

"I also saw someone I didn't recognize, but I think it might have been Donnie Ray Bryant," Carla says.

I look at Nell. "Could he have been coming from the theater when you saw him?"

"It's possible. I have no way of knowing for sure. It's possible he never even came in the house."

"Okay," Dad says, "I know we've been on here a while. Thank you all. If you think of anything else—anything at all, please let me, Merrill, John, or Gerald Woodson know. We'll be in touch as we have more questions. Be safe and stay well. We'll do our best to keep you up to date. I know some of you live outside my jurisdiction, but let me know if you feel like you need additional security, and I'll coordinate it with the other sheriff's departments."

TUESDAY, APRIL 14, 2020

Tuesday, April 14, 2020
604,165 confirmed cases and 25,776 deaths in the US

The United States passes Italy to become the country with the most coronavirus deaths, and all fifty states now report deaths.

Protests erupt over stay-at-home orders, including in Michigan, Kentucky, Oklahoma, and North Carolina.

After claiming total authority over the states a few days before, saying, "The president of the United States calls the shots," the President tweets: "LIBERATE MINNESOTA, LIBERATE MICHIGAN, " and "LIBERATE VIRGINIA."

32

———

Merrill and I are playing basketball on the outdoor court behind the high school—something we've been doing for several weeks since the old gym on Main Street was closed down in response to the coronavirus.

I rarely think of basketball without also thinking of Martin Fisher, but on an outdoor court like the one in the apartment complex we shared when I first moved to Atlanta, he absolutely haunts me.

Martin, a young kid who was largely left on his own, had become a kind of surrogate son to me—before eventually becoming the first victim in an investigation I was conducting and whose death was caused by my actions.

The sky is clear, the sun bright, the evening, apart from a small breeze, perfect for outdoor court basketball.

"Saw the video of you and your dad," Merrill says.

We each have our ball and are just shooting around and getting our own rebounds.

The video the woman in the car shot of Dad making his deputies take off their riot gear and put it in their trunks had made the rounds on social media—and had even been picked up by a few local and regional news outlets.

"He was even more impressive at Leviticus Lanier's church," I say, "but no one was recording—or if they were they haven't shared it yet."

"What I hear . . ." he says, "you the one who made the biggest difference there, but I'm glad he's sheriff again. That shit coulda gone all kinds of sideways. He showed a lot of wisdom and restraint and patience. Kind of leadership missing in most places these days. Need more like him."

"He actually asked me to mention to you that he's got an investigator position opening up he'd love for you to have," I say. "He's gonna talk to you when he sees you but wanted you to have some extra time to think about it. Said to tell you that you could keep your private agency and work cases for it on evenings and weekends."

He stops dribbling and holds the ball as he thinks about it, and I can tell from his expression that he's intrigued.

"Sounds like a best-of-both-worlds scenario," he says. "I had heard tell they exist, but . . . never believed it."

"It would be a sweet setup," I say. "And position you nicely to run for sheriff when he finally retires for good—which I think is what he has in the back of his mind."

"Always figured he had that in mind for you."

"Pretty sure I disabused him of that notion years ago."

He rolls his ball over beside the backboard's huge, black steel pole and we begin to rebound for each other, each of us taking turns shooting until we make five shots while the other one rebounds, then switching.

An outdoor court is not without its challenges. We are at the mercy of the elements—often unable to play because of rain, having to deal with shot-altering wind and blinding sun when we do. But it's not without its charms too. It's soothing and therapeutic on a soul level to be outside, close to the wooded area behind the school.

We had been forced to play here about a year and a half ago when, following Hurricane Michael, the old gym became a distribution center for emergency supplies, and we are familiar with and appreciative of this outdoor alternative that enables us to continue to practice this sport we both so love.

My phone begins to ring, and I run over to the open door of my truck to answer it.

It's Carla.

"Thanks for calling me back," I say.

"No problem," she says. "I got your message and you were right. I probably did make a face when Dixie said she was either in the kitchen or the bathroom all night—because I know for a fact she wasn't. She left the kitchen several times and it wasn't always to go to the bathroom in the hallway. I saw her all over the place as I was serving—including coming out of Jules's bedroom."

"Okay, thanks," I say. "That's very helpful."

"No problem," she says, "but . . . I really need the work she gives me . . . so, in case she's not a murderer, can you not tell her it was me who told you?"

"No problem," I say, repeating her oft-used phrase.

I end the call, place the phone back on the center console of my truck, and rejoin Merrill on the court.

"So," he says when it's my turn to shoot and he's standing beneath the goal to rebound for me, "ol' Hippie Nell goin' ahead with her b'day party?"

"Says so."

"What?" he says. "She figure she ain't got many more anyway, why not take the risk?"

I'm moving around, dribbling, running, shooting, practicing shot fakes, spin moves, and fadeaways, and my words come out in breathless bursts.

"I think she's not afraid of the virus because she's most likely had it already," I say. "She's taking an antibody test this week to confirm, but chances are good she got it on the cruise and that's what made her so sick when she got back. As far as being murdered . . . she says she won't eat or drink anything she's not absolutely certain about, knows it's the best way to catch the killer, and that we'll protect her."

I finish my five and we swap positions.

"Lavinia says she's not going under any circumstances," I say, "and Jules says she's going but wearing a mask and not eating or drinking anything."

"No guarantees the killer will use poison again," he says. "No way to guarantee their safety."

"That's what I told them," I say. "And they told me they were going to have it with or without us and don't hold us responsible for what happens, so we might as well be there to try and catch the killer."

"Can't you and Reggie shut it down?" he asks.

"Not before it happens and only while it's happening if there's more than ten people at a time, but we're not about to do that. We've had people getting together—mostly in their yards —since the quarantine started, and with a lot more than ten people."

"Hell," he says, "most folk 'round here actin' like there is no quarantine."

He's right. School's out. Churches and bars are closed. Events have been canceled. But otherwise small-town life in the rural South continues in a manner similar to pre-pandemic norms.

As I had hoped, Graham Arnold shuffles up as we're shooting.

"You ggg-guys playin' bbbb-basketball?"

"We are," I say. "Want to join us?"

"That's . . . okay. I'll jjjj-just watch."

He's a tall, thick, gangly white guy with thick glasses and a perpetually sunburned face. Awkward and childlike, he is mostly sweet and innocent, but can on occasion become inexplicably angry and agitated.

"Sorry we didn't get to visit more at Aunt Jules's birthday party," I say.

"I ate cake. Lots and lots of cccc-cake. It was good. Real gggg-good."

"Did you see what happened at the show in the theater?" I ask.

He frowns and shakes his enormous head. "No," he says, his voice full of sadness and regret, "T-Rex made me leave bbbb-before it . . . hhh-happened. Www-wish I had been there. Www-would have given them more medicine. Make them better."

"*More* medicine?" I ask. "Had you given them some before?"

He holds his finger over his lips. "T-Rex said don't tell."

"He didn't mean us," Merrill says. "You can tell us."

"Cccc-can't tell anyone. T-Rex said. Tttt-T-Rex is my bbbb-best friend."

"He's our friend too," Merrill says. "He wouldn't mind if you tell us."

"No," he says. "Hhhh-he's scared of yyy-you, MMMM-Merrill."

We try for a while longer, eventually even bribing him, but nothing works. Turns out Graham Arnold can be a secure vault with his information when he wants to be. So we decide to take a run at T-Rex instead.

33

———

I get T-Rex's number from a colleague in our narcotics unit and give him a call.

He doesn't answer.

Merrill and I are riding around looking for him at a few of his favorite haunts when Dad calls.

"Lillian was just attacked in her home," he says. "I'm headed over now. I'll meet you there. And bring Merrill if you can talk him into it."

Merrill glances over at me, raises his eyebrows, and gives me a *what's up* look when I end the call.

I tell him.

"Why would you have to talk me into going?" he says.

"She lives in Pine County," I say.

He laughs.

Several years ago, when Merrill and I were both still with the prison system, we worked a case that involved the corrupt sheriff of Pine County, Howard Hawkins, and Merrill had spent some time being tortured in a hidden cell in what the autocrat sheriff and his crooked family referred to as the dungeon.

"Only thing that'd make me want to go even more," he says, "is if Hawkins was still sheriff."

None of the Hawkinses are involved in the sheriff's department any longer, and Howard has been dead for a few years.

"I've heard good things about the sheriff they have now," I say.

"Yeah," Merrill says, "me too. Guess we 'bout to find out if they true."

By the time we reach Lillian's, the Pine County deputies who responded to the call are already gone, and we find Dad, Lavinia, and Lillian in her living room.

"You called them *too*?" Lillian asks.

"I'm afraid I did that," Dad says. "I just thought . . . based on what your grandma told me . . . that it was probably related to the case we're—"

"Grandma may have exaggerated," Lillian says.

"I most certainly did not," Lavinia says. "Honey, you were attacked."

"I was attempted attacked," she says.

"What happened?" I ask.

"Guy with a mask on tried to break into the back glass door," she says. "I heard him and called the police. I then went over, pulled back the curtain, and showed him my gun. That was it. Sorry y'all came out here for that."

"Could it be related to what happened to me, Jules, and Nell?" Lavinia asks.

"Did you recognize him?" Dad asks.

She shrugs. "He had a mask on and . . . like these dark blue coveralls or something and boots and gloves, but . . . I don't know . . . there was something the vaguest bit familiar about him. Maybe."

"What kind of mask was it?" I ask.

"Halloween."

"Do you mean Michael Myers, like in the movie *Halloween*, or just a Halloween trick-or-treat style mask?"

"Like a kid would wear at Halloween. It was grotesque. Creepy as hell. Like a cross between a pig and a man."

"Did he have a weapon?" Dad asks.

She shakes her head. "Not that I saw."

"Was he using a tool on the lock?"

She shakes her head.

"Was it Donnie Ray?" Lavinia asks. "Could you tell if—"

"I don't know. I just can't be sure."

"Was he the same size as Donnie Ray?" I ask.

"I think so," she says. "It was hard to tell. He was sort of hunched over working on the lock."

"He say anything?" Merrill asks. "Make any noises or gestures you recognized?"

She shakes her head. "No, not really. He did do this sort of weird thing when he saw me where he kind of tilted his head to the side. I've seen it done a lot in movies where the killer wears a mask. It's creepy because the mask doesn't change expressions, but . . . I don't know."

"You're moving in with me tonight," Lavinia says.

"Won't get any arguments from me," Lillian says.

"Is this something like Donnie Ray would do?" I ask. "The mask and costume, breaking in."

She shakes her head. "Not really, but the truth is I don't know him that well, and there's no telling what he'll do on some of the shit he does."

Merrill says, "Do you have a home security system that might have captured photos or video of him or did you get a picture with your phone?"

She shakes her head. "I don't have a system yet. But I will after this. Calling Simply Safe tonight—that's the one I hear all the ads for on the true crime podcasts I listen to. I should've taken a picture, but I was on the phone with the dispatcher and didn't think of it. Sorry."

"Got nothin' to be sorry about, missy," he says.

We wait while Lillian gathers some things to take to Lavinia's, and linger in the yard once they drive away.

Dad says, "Think it's connected to what happen to her grandma, Jules, and Nell?"

I shrug. "Could be. Hard to see how it's not—whether it's Donnie Ray or not. If it was him, he could've poisoned the honey. If it's not him, then it'd be too big a coincidence not to be connected."

"I agree," Dad says.

"Me three," Merrill says.

"Glad to have all of them over in our counties where we can keep a better eye on them," he says. "Need to let the others know so they can be even more careful."

"Oh, I'm sure they already know about this," I say.

"Need to warn Jasmine that he may not just be going after the mothers but the daughters too."

"Plan to call her as soon as we're done here."

"What does it say that he tried to break into her home?" he says. "That's a lot different than putting some poison in some honey."

"Unless that's all he was here to do," I say. "He didn't have a weapon."

"That she saw."

"And he ran away when he saw her . . . so maybe he was breaking in to poison something."

Dad says, "I wish to hell Nell would postpone her party."

"Me too," I say. "But since she won't, let's use it to catch him."

THURSDAY, APRIL 23, 2020

Thursday, April 23, 2020
861,551 confirmed cases and 44,038 deaths in the US

Nearly 14 percent of the US workforce has filed for unemployment over the past month.

At a White House press briefing, President Trump suggests exploring the injecting of disinfectant and bright light as a way of combatting the coronavirus.

The House of Representatives approves an additional relief bill to help small businesses and hospitals. Earlier funds for small businesses were taken by large corporations.

President Trump says his administration is conducting "serious investigations" into China's handling of the disease outbreak, and would most likely seek "very substantial" damages from Beijing over the pandemic.

34

"You want us to admit we crashed," Carson Gibson is saying. "We crashed. Okay? But that's all we did, and we wouldn't've done that if we had known somebody was gonna poison somebody, but it sure as shit wasn't us."

I'm at Carson and Sue Ann Gibson's redbrick ranch home in the Whispering Pines subdivision. I'm in the yard a good twelve feet away from them. They're standing on the porch. I'm wearing a mask, which means even though talking loudly, I'm difficult to hear and understand.

"Why'd you do it?" I ask.

"He did it for me," Sue Ann says. "I'd never been to one of their shindigs and when I told him I was disappointed that I never would get to, he suggested we crash."

Hurricane Michael mercifully left a few trees in the Gibsons' yard, and we're surrounded by tall, narrow pines whose tops reach high into and vanish in the evening sky above.

"Under ordinary circumstances," he says, "we'd've gone virtually unnoticed, but given the damn virus and then somebody trying to bump off the old broads . . ."

"We have nothing against them," Sue Ann says. "To tell the truth I feel sorry for Nell. Her life hasn't gone so good since Carson left her for me. She's kooky, sort of crazy and all, but she's not too bad. I find the other two harder to take—sort of uppity and all, but even they aren't *too* bad. Can't imagine why anyone would want to kill them. They seem more harmless— even silly—than anything else."

Carson says, "If I'm being completely transparent, I didn't just do it for Sue Ann. I always enjoyed their parties when I was with Nell, and I missed them and thought it would be fun to crash."

"Are you saying you don't benefit in any way from Nell's death?" I ask.

He lets out a little laugh. "You mean apart from outliving her when I've subsisted on red meat and fried potatoes and she's always done all that hippie shit?"

I don't respond.

"I'm not sure," he adds, "but I believe we still own a little property together and there may be a little insurance or something, but nothing that amounts to much of anything—if it did, we would've already split it up."

"All your assets weren't divided in the divorce?" I ask.

"You're talkin' about Hippie Nell," he says. "We never officially got married or divorced. She doesn't believe in marriage any more than she believes in the other things normal people do. We had a hippie dippie ceremony in the woods and when we went our separate ways we had what she called a mindful uncoupling. Can you beat it? *A mindful uncoupling.*"

"So you do benefit financially from her death?" I say.

"Not in any kind of way that amounts to anything," he says.

35

Max Reynolds is the kind of man who acts as if he has money but is actually not just broke but heavily in debt.

Though it's more his attitude and how he carries himself, he only wears expensive clothes and drives the latest model year of the most tricked-out truck Chevy offers. Even his after-shave has the exclusive health club smell of money and success.

I finally catch up with him as he's loading the last of his things into the back of his truck in Lavinia's yard.

"Take that ridiculous thing off," he says, nodding toward my mask. "You're ten feet away for Chrissakes."

"I can't," I say. "I'm required to wear it on duty—but I'd wear it anyway. I'm coming in contact with too many people right now. I don't want to wind up being an unwitting carrier."

"Well, I wouldn't be caught dead in one of those silly things," he says. "And I'll be fine—as will most strong red-blooded Americans."

"It's not the strong and healthy we're doing it for," I say. "Trying to protect the weak and elderly."

"Y'all are all making a big deal over nothin," he says. "But even if you weren't . . . the herd has to be thinned occasionally. This is nature's way of strengthening us. Coddling and catering to the weak only makes us all weaker. Anyway, what's your question? I need to go unload this shit before it gets too late."

"Everyone was surprised to see you at Jules's birthday party, since you and Lavinia are split up," I say. "I was just wondering what you were doing there."

"Where I go and why I go there is my business," he says. "I'm an American citizen and I'm free to do whatever I want to whenever I want to."

Though what he's saying isn't true—he's not free to do anything he wants to—and even though he doesn't afford that same sentiment to all American citizens, namely those in the minority who don't look like, dress like, believe like, and worship like him, I know to challenge him on it would be a waste of time and a path that would lead us away from why I'm here to get into it.

"I'm not questioning your freedoms," I say. "I'm just asking why you chose to do what you did with them that particular night."

"I'm under no obligation to tell you," he says. "I know my rights."

"You're right," I say. "You're under no obligation to talk to me at all."

"Not sayin' I won't talk to you," he says. "Just want it crystal clear that I don't have to. I know my rights, and not you or anyone else will tread on them."

"Have no intention to," I say. "But I'm curious . . . do those same rights extend to everyone?"

"Every law-abiding American citizen. Not some damn dirty illegal, but true Americans, yeah."

Leave it there, John. Remember why you're here. Ask your questions. Get your answers. Don't get into—

"Young black men as much as any other American citizen?" I ask, unable to help myself.

"Not thugs, criminals, carjackers, rapists and drug dealers, but law-abiding American citizens."

Let it go, John. Don't sabotage your own interview. What's wrong with you?

"Why did you jump to thugs, rapists, and drug dealers when I mentioned young black men?"

He shakes his head. "I know you," he says. "And I know your type. I know who your friends are and who you sympathize with. I ain't about to get into this with you."

At least one of you can show a little restraint.

"You want me to tell you about that party or not?" he says.

"Please."

"This is off the record," he says.

I'm not a reporter. I have no off the record, but don't mention it.

"So I better not see this in any newspaper story or hear it on the street," he continues, "but if Lavinia and I were already done at that point, it's news to me. I knew we were having a little trouble, but I didn't know it was over. I don't think it was then. If I had, I sure as shit wouldn't've gone to that stupid party. But Lavinia was always complaining that I never did any of the things she liked. Never went shopping or out to eat or to her silly concerts or the stupid parties with her friends. All I did was watch ballgames and fish and hang out with my buddies, so I made an effort. That's all. It was a gesture. Turns out it was too little too late, but there it is. That's why I was there. I wish I hadn't've gone. And I'll tell you another thing. I ain't the least bit broken up about this. Lavinia ain't an easy woman to live with. I promise you that. So I won't miss her negative, complaining ass not one little bit, I can tell you that."

"What about her negative complaining ass's money?" I ask. "Will you miss that?"

. . .

"HOW ARE YOU?" I ask Lillian.

We are standing out in her grandmother's front yard. She had walked out when Max drove away.

"I'm okay," she says. "Better some days than others—some moments than others. Doing okay right now."

"Nothing else has happened?" I ask. "No contact of any kind from Donnie Ray?"

She nods. "Nothing. None."

"How is it being here with your grandmother?"

She smiles. "Challenging. Worse 'cause I can't go to work. Global pandemic is not the time to have to move back home."

"Sorry," I say. "Hope it's temporary."

"Not as much as me."

"If you ever need to get away for a while, we have a spare room you're welcome to."

"Thank you," she says. "I appreciate that. And I may just take you up on it sometime."

"I hope you will."

"How'd it go with Max?" she asks.

I shake my head and frown. "Not well. I blew it. Let my ego get the better of me."

"Well, it doesn't matter," she says. "There's just no way it was him. He's an ignorant, bigoted asshole, but he's no killer."

We each drift off into ourselves.

"Grandma is not going to Nell's party," she says. "Feels guilty as hell but believes it's too risky on both fronts—though she won't admit that the virus has anything to do with it."

"She's in a high-risk demographic," I say.

"Yeah, old as fuck. Same is true for Nellie Bell and Jules, but . . . Anyway, I plan to go to represent our family, and I was just wondering if you and Merrill might keep an extra eye on me.

I'm not going to eat or drink anything, but if it's Donnie . . . he'll probably come at me with a knife."

"We're going to have extra protection there and will definitely keep a close eye on you, though I wish you'd sit this one out. We're gonna do our best to protect everyone but we can't guarantee that no one will get hurt or worse."

"Yeah," she says, "it's a bad idea all the way around. So many things can go wrong and only one thing can go right. Well, two. I was thinking catching him, but I guess it'll all be considered a success if we all survive."

SATURDAY, APRIL 25, 2020

Saturday, April 25, 2020
1,000,000 confirmed cases and 60,000 deaths in the US

36

———————

The tops of the cypress trees emerging from the black water give the Dead Lakes the appearance of a submerged city, hinting at the mystery of what lies beneath.

The covered wooden dock near the base of West Arm Creek bridge extends out onto the Dead Lakes and is surrounded and canopied by a thick, watery cypress tree forest.

It's evening. The elongated shadows of afternoon have softened into evening, suffusing everything with a dusky glow and quiet calm.

String lights and soft music add to the ambience of elegant outdoor dinner party.

There are more people in attendance at Nell's party than I expected, but far fewer than at Jules's and far, far fewer than normally attend.

Because Nell's small, rundown place is not only still blue-roofed and plywood-patched from Hurricane Michael but also not large or posh enough for a party like this, her birthday is taking place at the home of Ryan Harrison, a longtime friend and fan of the Tupelo Queens who is sheltering in place with his grown children in Jacksonville.

To accommodate safety and social distancing, an event tent has been set up in the backyard about thirty feet from the entrance to the wooden walkway that leads out to the dock. The fewer than twenty partygoers, who are mostly practicing social distancing, are divided among the dock and the tent and the area between the two. Only the serving staff have masks on.

Dad and I and two undercover deputies roam the crowd, alert for anything suspicious, as assigned bodyguards remain with the two Queens in attendance wherever they go—Merrill with Jules, Jake with Nell.

An event like this wouldn't take places in many other parts of the country and world right now, but most of our neighbors here in the rural South think our practice of wearing masks and social distancing are unnecessary and even absurd.

Scanning the sparse and spread-out crowd, I try to note who is here who was also at Jules's party.

Carla is once again working the party, but with a different caterer. Dixie Ledoux, who is in attendance as a guest, has been replaced by Charles Harbuck, Nell's cousin who she says she trusts more than anyone on the planet.

Nell's family is here—Jasmine, Nash, and Harley Carter. And Paul Branch is with them.

Lillian Pritchett is present. As is Max Reynolds.

Mama Monroe is again helping with food prep.

Zaire is here with Merrill.

Anna and our girls are not in attendance—something we agreed would be best under the circumstances.

I'm surprised to see Carson and Sue Ann Gibson, but even more surprised to see T-Rex.

I have been trying to track him down since Merrill and I had talked to Graham on at the outdoor basketball court, but hadn't been able to find him.

I walk over to where he and Graham Arnold are standing on the far left side of the dock.

"Why won't you take my calls?" I ask. "Or at least return my messages."

Rex Anthony Spears is an albino man with a big belly and short, dinosaur-like arms, perpetually in a wife beater and jogging pants, an excessive amount of gaudy gold chains hanging around his thick neck.

He is watching as two good-sized gators approach the dock, only their eyes and the tops of their heads visible as they glide through the inky waters.

"Been busy," he says. "Thinkin' 'bout getting a secretary to handle shit for me."

"I cccc-could do it," Graham says.

"No you couldn't," he says. "You're too retarded."

"*Hey*," I say. "That's not cool. Don't call him that."

"I'm nnn-not too retarded," Graham says. "I cool cool ccc-could do it."

"You're never still," T-Rex says. "Always movin'. Besides with your stu-stu-stuttering it'd take you forever to ttt-take a mmm-messsage."

"I said don't talk to him like that," I say.

Graham responds to the tone in my voice and my change in body language.

"Hey," he says, stepping in between us, "don't talk to my bbbb-best friend like that."

"It's okay, big fella," T-Rex says. "He just wants to make sure nobody's picking on you."

Graham steps back over to where he had been.

"I'm good to him," T-Rex says. "Treat him better than anybody. He's my best friend and I'm his. And I can call him a retard for the same reason blacks can call each other the n-word. I'm a little retarded too. So, what'd you want to see me about? You've taken enough of our time."

"Why were you at Jules's party?" I ask.

"Same reason I'm at this one."

"Graham said y'all put some medicine into their honey?"

"Their *honey? Whaaa*? No idea what he meant. Ain't put nothin' in nobody's honey. Maybe he said money and you mmm-misunderstood him."

"What medicine did you give them?" I ask.

"There is no *them*," he says. "Only Nell."

"Only Nell what?"

"I only supply Nell," he says. "I have a license and she has a subscription."

"A prescription?"

"Yeah, that," he says. "Only to her. Not even her daughter. She's nuttier than Nell. I sell to Nell, she shares with her daughter. But I don't put the herb in her honey. I put it in her hand— just like she does my money."

"Nell's medicine is her weed," I say. "And you only sell to her. I mean out of the Queens. And that's why you were at Jules's party and why you're at this one."

37

<hr>

"**I**s the birthday girl enjoying herself?" I ask.

I find Nell over by the food prep station on the far side of the event tent.

She looks radiant in her vintage paisley floral print sleeveless mini dress with the deep V.

Jake has taken this opportunity to go the restroom—a blue "His" port-a-potty next to the pink "Hers" on the backside of the yard near the tree line.

"I am," she says.

"Groovy dress," I say. "You look amazing."

"I feel amazing. Everything is just . . . splendid. Couldn't be happier."

"Unless you had Grandma here to argue with," Lillian says, joining us.

Unlike Nell, Lillian neither looks happy nor dressed for a party.

"That's true," Nell says, "but I'm so happy you came. Makes my night."

I say, "I'm sure it was difficult to come. I know you're still grieving and then to undergo that awful attack. But I'm so glad you came."

"I'm afraid I can't argue with you like she does," Lillian says, "but I'm honored to represent our family for you. I'm not a Queen but I'll do my best to be a good Tupelo Princess."

"You're the best one," Nell says, "just don't tell my Jasmine I said so."

"I know Grandma can come across as rigid and gruff, but . . . she really feels bad about not being here."

"Oh, I know," Nell says, gesturing to her dress. "She paid a small fortune for this little vintage beautyto help assuage her guilt."

Nell's catering cousin comes up beside her and says, "No one's eating or drinking much of anything."

"Can you blame them," Nell says. "Charles, this is my goddaughter Lillian Pritchett, and Jules's nephew John Jordan. Lilly and John, this is my oldest and dearest cousin, Charles."

He's a slight, oddly shaped little man with sun-damaged skin, a lisp he seems self-conscious about, and what might be a toupee. His once white apron and pristine hot-sauce-patterned chef pants are smeared and soiled and stained with many of the ingredients of his culinary creations, his black gloves and mask dusted with powdered sugar.

He starts to extend his hand as he steps toward us, but then realizes what he's doing and stops. "Pandemic greetings," he says, nodding. "Nice to meet you both."

"Nice to meet you," we both say.

"I better get back to it," he says, "but . . . I'm afraid we're gonna have a lot of very good food go to waste."

"I don't know," Nell says, "Graham and T-Rex are doin' their part."

"Please spread the word that I am personally tasting everything we serve and will be happy to do it in front of anyone. No one is coming near my food except me and Ms. Monroe, so it's safe. I'm guaranteeing it with my life."

He rejoins Mama Monroe over behind the tables of buffet trays and warmers.

"I'm surprised to see T-Rex here," I say.

"Why?" she asks. "You don't invite your pharmacists to your parties?"

"So he is your supplier?" I ask. "Graham said something about them giving you medicine and I wanted to make sure it wasn't poison."

"He is and I assure you he wouldn't bump off his best customer."

Lillian says, "I can't believe Carson and Sue Ann crashed again."

"They didn't," Nell says. "I invited them."

"You *did*?" she says.

"Tried to invite everyone who was at Jules's party—even Tom and Randall, though I'm not sure they'll come. I figure it's the best way to catch whoever's trying to hurt us."

"But—" Lillian begins.

"Let me tell you something," Nell says. "I've never felt safer in all my life—all y'all here looking out for me, and this ol' hippie has a few tricks up her sleeve as well, but the God's Gospel is . . . I'm not afraid of dying. I will soon anyway, and if that's what it takes to catch the killer and keep the rest of you safe, sign me up."

"Aunt Nell, that's so . . . incredibly sweet—and brave and noble, but let's not let it come to that, okay?"

"I don't intend to. I most surely do not."

38

———

"How's it going?" I ask.

Nash shrugs, but doesn't say anything.

I find him alone near the water's edge between the dock and the bridge, drawing designs and patterns on the black surface with a long, skinny oak branch.

"How's the guitar playing going?"

"Okay, I guess," he says.

"I wanna hear you play sometime when you're up for it," I say.

He doesn't respond.

"You okay?"

He shrugs again.

"What's going on?"

Again the shrug.

He's yet to look at me or even glance in my direction.

"What is it, man? What's wrong?"

"Just sort of sick of all the shit," he says.

"Any shit in particular?" I ask.

"Just everything, all the bullshit. This bullshit party. Mom being here with fuckin' Paul like we're some sort of normal family or something. So sick of all the fake bullshit."

"The world's full of that," I say. "People don't know who they are, so they pretend. Or they're insecure about who they are so they pretend to be what they think other people will like —and other people are mostly worried about themselves and how they come across."

"Makes me tired."

I nod as I think about how tiring and tiresome inauthenticity is.

"I know I keep saying it, but you get to choose the type of person you want to be. You get to be real, true to yourself and what's important to you."

"Is my grandma going to die?" he asks.

"We've got a lot of good people trying to prevent that from happening," I say, turning back toward the crowd and trying to spot Nell.

"If I tell you something, will you swear not to tell anybody I told you?" he asks.

I nod. "Of course."

"She tested positive," he says.

"For?"

"She took another test," he says. "Different kind. Antibiotic or—"

"Antibody," I say. "Shows if you've ever had it. The other one just shows if you have it when you take it."

"She has the virus or had it or whatever," he says. "Hasn't taken anything but her hippie home remedies and she's out here infecting everybody."

"I appreciate you letting me know," I say. "I really do. I won't ever say I heard it from you."

"They don't know I know," he says. "I just happened to overhear her and Mom talkin' about it. Mom didn't even tell Paul."

"I'm gonna go check on things," I say. "You wanna walk up with me?"

"I'm good."

"Wanna ask your Mom if you can stay with us tonight?" I ask.

He lights up for the first time since we started talking. "I brought some clothes and my guitar just in case you asked."

"You don't have to wait for me to ask," I say. "You can come over any time you like. I was thinking . . . We can turn that room into yours if you'd like to."

"Really? Cool."

"Be thinking about what you'd like in it and we'll set it up and decorate it like you want it."

39

———

As I make my way back up to the party, I see that Tom and Randall decided to put in an appearance after all. They have Jules cornered near the pump house, not far from the event tent.

"Can I have your attention please," Nell says.

She is standing close to the entry of the walkway that leads out to the dock, angled so she's speaking to the guests on the dock, in the tent, and in the area between the two.

"I want to say how much I appreciate you all making the effort to be here for my birthday—especially given the current state of affairs. And given that—and because I don't want to put anyone at any more undue risk than I already have, I figured we should make an early night of it."

My heart starts racing as Carla, Mama Monroe, and Charles Harbuck begin passing out glasses of champagne.

"If Jules will join me over here, we'll have a toast and do a quick a cappella number for you."

Jules extricates herself from the Foster brothers and makes her way over to Nell.

"Feel free not to drink the toast," Nell says, "but if you'll direct your attention over to Charles, he's going to do a little demonstration for you."

With everyone watching, Charles pours some champagne from the bottle he's holding into one of the glasses on his tray. He then has Carla and Mama Monroe pour some from the bottles they have into the same glass and drinks it.

"I wouldn't serve you fine folks anything I wouldn't drink or eat myself," he says.

The three servers then continue to distribute the glasses and everyone prepares for the toast.

"We've been through so very much together," Jules says. "Never a global pandemic and someone trying to punch our ticket, but . . . still, an awful lot. Nellie Bell is not like a sister to me. She is my sister. Just as Lavinia is—who is represented here tonight by her beautiful granddaughter, Lilly. I just wanted to say that I can't imagine how less my life would have been without you in it, my dear, dear friend. Tonight I drink to you, your life, your birthday, and to the hope that when we celebrate it next year, all of these current trials will be all but forgotten. Please raise your glass with me, everyone. To our Nellie Bell. Many happy returns."

Both Nell and Jules raise their glasses, clink them together, then toss their contents over their shoulders.

Most everyone present follows suit, though a few actually take a sip.

"Happy Birthday," Jules says. "What ditty do you want us to do?"

As Nell tries to respond, nothing comes out, and her eyes grow wide in panic as she grabs her throat and then her chest and falls to the ground, convulsing.

Zaire is on the ground beside her in seconds.

Dad calls for an ambulance as everyone else looks on in shock.

It's obvious from the way her body is contorting and the sounds she's making that Nell can't breathe.

"But she didn't drink any of the champagne," someone in the crowd says.

A few of the people who drank the toast move away from the crowd and force themselves to vomit.

As everyone watches and waits and Zaire works on Nell, no one develops any other symptoms apart from sympathy vomiting.

Soon even Nell's symptoms are gone.

By the time the ambulance arrives less than five minutes later, she is dead.

40

"MAMA," Jasmine is yelling. "MAMA. WAKE UP."

She is down on the ground, screaming and crying and yelling, trying to shake her mother awake as Zaire tries to restrain her.

Jules reaches down and touches her shoulder. "She's gone, dear. I'm so sorry."

Jasmine jerks away from Jules. "NO," she yells again. "MAMA. MAMA, WAKE UP. You can't be gone."

Dad and I get on either side of Jasmine and gently pull her back.

"NO," she yells as us. "NO."

"She's gone," Dad says.

"NO."

"I'm so sorry," I say.

"There's nothing we can do for her now," Dad says. "Except figure out what happened to her. Let's let the doctors and EMTs and medical examiner do that, okay?"

"NO."

Paul comes up and takes her, wrapping her up in a hug and pulling her to him and away from us and the rest of the crowd.

Several feet behind him Nash is holding Harley. I make eye contact with him and mouth *Sorry. You okay?*

He nods.

"But she didn't drink anything," Jasmine says. "We all saw. She didn't drink anything."

"I know, baby, I know," Paul says.

She snatches her head up from his chest and whips it around toward us. "How could y'all let this happen? You were supposed to be protecting her. How?"

"We're going to figure that out," Dad says. "We don't even know what happened yet. It looked like a heart attack. We've got to find that out first. Let's let the medical people find that out and then we'll go from there."

"I hope it was a heart attack," she says. "I really do. Because if y'all let someone kill her ..."

41

"It looked like a heart attack," Zaire is saying, "but I'll bet you my sweet black ass it wasn't."

"*Whoa*," Merrill says. "Hold up. That's not your sweet black ass to bet. It's mine. Bet something else."

"I bet you Merrill's sweet black ass it wasn't," she says.

"Wait, what?" Merrill says.

The three of us are standing apart from the crowd, waiting for the arrival of Reggie, the ME, and the FDLE crime scene unit.

"Poison?" I ask her.

She nods.

"We all saw her not drink the champagne," Merrill says. "And she said she wasn't going to eat or drink anything all night."

I nod. "We need to find out if she stuck to that."

Zaire says, "If she was poisoned . . . it wasn't the same type used in the first attempt."

I raise my eyebrows. "Interesting," I say.

"Why's that?" Merrill says.

"Why use two different poisons?"

"The first one didn't work so well," he says.

I nod. "Could certainly just come down to that, but . . . if there's another reason . . . it could possibly point to who's responsible."

Merrill looks at Zaire. "What kind of poison makes some-body look like they're havin' a heart attack?"

"Quite a few," she says. "But I'd say the top two candidates are cyanide and fentanyl."

"How difficult are they to get?" I ask.

"Not hard at all," she says. "Hell, you can order them online. And it wouldn't take much for it to work. But—and this might help with who's responsible—the person handling them would have to be extremely careful. It'd be easy to kill yourself instead of or in addition to your intended victim."

"If that's the case, that's also interesting," I say. "Very inter-esting. And that wasn't true of the previous poison used, was it?"

42

"How the hell did that happen right under our noses?" Dad is saying. "We were right here. She was never by herself, was she?"

He looks at Jake.

Jake shakes his head. "Never left her unless somebody else was with her."

"*Somebody*?" Dad says.

"One of you," he says. "Went to take a leak when John was with her and to grab a drink when you were with her. That was it."

"Okay," Dad says. "Good. Maybe it was just a heart attack."

"Zaire doesn't think so," I say.

"Really? Well, hell."

We are quiet a moment as they take that in.

Around us partygoers are giving statements and being allowed to leave. Everyone has been moved up into the side yard of the house, away from where the ME is working on the body and FDLE is processing the scene.

Dad looks at Jake. "Did she eat—"

Reggie walks up. "Gentlemen," she says.

We nod and speak to her.

Reggie Summers, the first female sheriff of Gulf County, is a thick, muscular cowgirl of a woman, perpetually in faded blue jeans and round-toe roper boots. As usual, her long, straight hair is pulled back in a ponytail.

"This is . . ." she says. "I don't have the words for what this is. Zaire thinks she was poisoned and the ME says he's inclined to agree. And—if they're all related—then we've got attempted murder in Potter County, attempted B and E in Pine County, and now murder in Gulf County. Gonna take some cooperation and—"

"You've got it from me," Dad says. "And from what I've seen, the new sheriff in Pine County is a good guy."

"I've had more trouble with good guys in my life than bad ones," she says with a smile, "but maybe this will be different."

"If Nell was murdered, then this takes precedence over everything else," Dad says.

She nods. "Thanks, Jack, but I plan to coordinate with you on everything. Not only did this start in your county, but it involves your family."

"Wonder why Jules wasn't poisoned," I say. "I mean if Nell was. Why not Jules too? Did the killer try and fail? Did she not give him or her the opportunity? Or was he only targeting Nell tonight? I wish we knew for sure that Nell was poisoned, but assuming she was . . . Is it possible that the plan was to kill each Queen on her birthday and Jules was the intended victim at her birthday and something went wrong?"

"Did I hear my name?" Jules asks, stepping over to us.

"Are you sure you're okay?" Dad asks her again.

"I'm wrecked," she says. "I can't believe my Nellie Bell is really gone, but . . . I'm fine physically. Lavinia was right—we should've never been here tonight. It's just that Nell was so certain she'd be okay. I really believed she would be or I wouldn't've been here. I—"

Lillian steps over to Jules, holding out her phone. "Grandma wants to speak to you," she says. "I've just told her about Aunt Nell."

Jules takes the phone and steps a few more feet away from us.

"I still can't believe she's gone," Lillian says, shaking her head slowly. "Doesn't seem real. I know I'm in shock, but it really doesn't."

"I know," I say. "I'm so sorry we let this happen."

"I don't think y'all *let* anything happen," she says. "I'm not sure what else you could've done—except prevent her from having the party. And I'm not sure anyone could've done that. I know Grandma and Jules sure tried."

Jules steps back over and hands Lillian her phone. "I heard the tail end of that," she says, "and y'all have nothin' to apologize for. If Nell was killed—and we still don't know that she was for sure—that's on her, just as it's on me for being here. If something happened to me I wouldn't blame y'all, and if someone did something to Nell she wouldn't blame y'all either. She said as much several times leading up to this. She was just so certain she'd be okay. I've never seen her so sure about anything. And she didn't drink the champagne. Neither of us did. So it must have been a heart attack or something. It was all just too much for her dear old heart."

"Did you eat or drink anything at all tonight?" Dad asks.

She shakes her head. "Not a bite. Not a drop. Except . . ."

"Except what?" he says. "Did Nell?"

She looks at Jake and the rest of us follow her gaze.

"Did she eat or drink anything at any point tonight?" Dad asks. "What's going on?"

Jake looks back at Jules.

"Jules," Dad says.

"Nell did her own little champagne toast before the one with everyone," she says, "but she went to her locked car and got the bottle and glasses out and opened it herself. And we all drank from the same bottle, so . . ."

"Who is *we*?" Dad says.

"It was all at Nell's insistence," she says. "It was her bottle and glasses and it stayed locked in her car and she opened and poured. Said she wasn't about to let some silly threat break over fifty years of tradition. And we all drank it and we're all fine."

"Who?" Dad says again.

"Me," she says. "And Jake and Charles and Lillian, who stood in for her grandmother. She tried to include Jasmine but couldn't find her."

Dad turns to Jake. "You not only let her do it but drank with her?"

"Wasn't about to let Aunt Jules drink something I wasn't willing to. And the point is we're all fine."

Dad looks at Lillian.

"I couldn't say no to her," she says. "And the truth is . . . God, Grandma would be mortified if she finds out any of this . . . But the truth is . . . I'm having a hard time caring if I live or not right now."

43

When Mama Monroe tells us that Charles Harbuck is in the restroom and has been for a while, my first thought is we might be about to find a second victim, but as we head over to the port-a-potty, he emerges from it before we get there.

"You okay?" Reggie asks.

"Yeah," he says, wiping tears from his red eyes, "why?"

"Thought you might be sick."

"Only with grief," he says.

"You mind joining us to walk through the little private toast y'all had at Nell's car?"

He shakes his head. "Not at all."

He joins us and we walk over to the large front yard where the vehicles are parked.

One of the first to arrive, Nell has parked her old white Honda Accord near the front far corner of the house.

When we reach it, Reggie says, "No one but John touch anything."

I slip on latex gloves and try the handle. It's locked.

"Who has the key?" Dad asks.

Jules says, "Nell did. Must still be on her."

As Reggie radios a deputy to see if the ME will check Nell's pockets for the key, Dad says, "Okay, take us through it."

"Nell just walked by with Jake and Charles and said come with me," Jules says.

"Same for me," Lillian says, "but she sort of motioned to me."

"She pulled me off a ham I was carving and ordered me to come with her," Charles says. "I've never said *no* to her, and I wasn't about to on her birthday."

"None of you knew ahead of time this was going to happen?" Reggie says.

They each confirm they didn't.

"She didn't tell us what we were doing until we got here," Jules says.

"What exactly did she say?" Dad asks.

"She said, 'I'll be damned if I'm gonna break a fifty-year tradition 'cause someone might want me dead.' She then explained how she had hidden her own bottle of champagne and glasses in the trunk and how she had just bought it today and there was no way anyone could've poisoned it, so would we please join her for a toast and would Lillian stand in for Lavinia."

A deputy walks up with a clear evidence bag containing Nell's car key on a tie-dyed peace symbol key chain and hands it to Reggie.

"Thank you, Steve," she says as he turns and walks away.

She hands the key to me and I open the bag just enough for the key to fit into the lock and unlock the door.

Returning the key fully into the bag and closing it, I take a look around.

The car is empty.

"It's not here," I say.

"Sorry, no," Jules says. "It was all in the trunk and she put it back in there when we were finished. I guess I thought you were opening the car to pop the trunk."

"And she did all that while y'all were watching?" Reggie asks. "Unlocked the door, popped the trunk."

Jules nods. "She had lost her fob a long time ago. Always had to use the key itself."

I say, "And she opened the door and popped the trunk from inside instead of using the key directly on the trunk?"

"Yeah," Jake says.

I reach down and pop the trunk and we all move to the back of the car.

Since Dad, Reggie, and Jake still don't have gloves on, I lift the trunk and we all look inside.

There in an otherwise spotless trunk is an empty bottle of champagne, lying next to an ice bucket, the discarded wire muselet, the cork, and five glasses.

Reggie radios for FDLE to come process the car and bag the bottle, glasses, muselet, and cork for analysis.

"And you all drank?" Dad asks.

They all indicate they did.

"Did Nell have more than the rest of you?" he asks.

"I'd say she had less than anyone else," Jules says.

"When she started pouring it," Charles says, "I stopped her and told her I wanted to drink it first and to wait a few moments to make sure it was okay before anyone else had any."

"That was very noble of you," Reggie says.

"I'm an old man. I've lived a good life. I adore dear Nell and would do anything I could to protect her. It's what I told her I insisted on doing when she asked me to cater her party. Told her I'd only agree to it if she'd agree to let me taste test everything so no one could say any of my food or drink hurt anyone. And I did it and she died anyway."

"What happened next?" Reggie asks.

"It was all very quick," Jules says. "I made a toast, we all clicked glasses, drank, then Charles and I returned everything to the trunk, and we all made our way back over to the party for the official toast. And y'all all know what happened after that—though I still can't believe it."

44

———

"I should've been here," Lavinia is saying. "Are you sure you're okay?"

Lillian and Jules reassure her again that they are fine.

She had arrived a few minutes before and rushed over to her granddaughter and remaining best friend, looking as if she rolled straight out of bed to do so.

"Poor Nellie Bell," she says. "I can't believe she's gone—and that I wasn't here for her."

"Let's face it," Jules says, "you're a selfish bitch. Always have been."

Everyone laughs a little uncomfortably.

"I am," Lavinia says. "I know you were kidding, but I really am."

"I wasn't kidding," Jules says. "And while we're on the subject of you . . . Doesn't matter what kind of emergency it is, a Tupelo Queen never leaves her house without makeup on."

"I must look a hot mess," she says. "Bet I could haunt a house, but I don't care. I just care about y'all—that y'all are alive. That's all that matters."

"It ain't *all* that matters," Jules says. "You look like you been rode hard and put up wet."

It's later. Most everyone but law enforcement is gone.

"Poor Jasmine," Lavinia says. "She must be an absolute basket case."

"The EMTs gave her something to calm her down," Lillian says. "Put her out cold. May be the first Western medicine she's ever had."

"Poor dear," Lavinia says again. "But it's not her first meds. Nell didn't know, but Paul talked her into taking anti-depressants. Now, please tell me . . . Who the hell is trying to kill us and why?"

"We don't know," Jules says. "But whoever it is better hope the police find him before I do."

"How'd they get Nell and not you?" she asks.

"We're not sure—really of anything yet. We don't even know for certain that she didn't die of natural causes."

"It's just not real. It can't be. I should've never let you come—either of you."

"We're grown ass women," Lillian says. "You couldn't've stopped us any more than you could have Nell."

"I could've tried harder," she says. "Done something. Call in a bomb threat or something. Should've called the authorities and told them y'all had the 'rona."

"Speaking of," Jules says, "I heard Nell did."

"What?" Lavinia says. "Really?"

"Yep."

"But she was tested," she says. "We all were. And we all came back negative."

"She took another test," Jules says. "More accurate. Came back positive."

"*No.*"

"Yep. Think all it meant was that she had had it. Not that

she necessarily had it now. But I don't know for sure. It's all so confusing."

"Is it possible she died of that instead of . . ." Lavinia asks.

"I guess it's possible," Jules says. "She was having a hard time breathing."

"I'm exhausted," Lillian says. "Can we go?"

"Of course," Lavinia says. "Sorry."

"Mind if I come with y'all?" Jules asks. "I really don't want to stay alone tonight."

"Was just about to ask you to," Lavinia says. "And I feel like we need to be there when Jasmine wakes up in the morning."

"I'll have a deputy escort you and stay there with you tonight," I say. "I'll touch base with you in the morning. Try to get some sleep. And, again, I'm so sorry about Aunt Nell."

45

———

"**I** don't care what anybody says," Dad says, "we're responsible for what happened to Nell."

I nod. "Yes we are."

As I pull the latex gloves out of my pocket, I realize I still have the small evidence bag with the car key in it.

We are searching Nell's little house, which isn't going to take long.

"I don't see it that way," Reggie says, "but I understand the sentiment. Thing is it's hard to see how it could've happened. It really could be a heart attack or related to the coronavirus. And you're not responsible if it was that."

"That's the frustrating part," Dad says. "We won't know for a while if she was poisoned or not—and if she was, how."

I nod. "I say we work it like a homicide until we know differently. That way we don't lose any time."

"Agreed," Reggie says.

"Work the statements," I say. "Conduct interviews. Come up with possible theories and motives. All the while protecting Jules, Lavinia, Lillian, and Jasmine."

Dad nods. "We do need to add Jasmine to that list."

"We've already got a deputy over at her house," Reggie says.

Inside the boarded-up windows and beneath the blue tarps blowing in the breeze on the roof, the small, old wooden house is damp and smells of mildew.

"This is so sad," Reggie says.

"I had no idea she was living this way," I say.

We have already searched the bedroom, bathroom, spare bedroom, and her arts and crafts room she used primarily for making jewelry, and are now back in the kitchen, dining, and den area.

Dad says, "I guarantee no one did. Think about how much Jules and Lavinia have helped her. They would've had this repaired a long time ago if they had known. She must have kept everyone away. I remember Jules mentioning something about her fighting with her insurance company like everybody else."

It's hard to tell what is the result of the hurricane or poverty and what are the lifestyle choices of an ancient, true-blue hippie chick, but there is no television, no computer, no microwave, and though she has an old cell she used from time to time, her main means of communication is the old beige desk telephone with the gray-buttoned number pad and the landline connected to it.

The furniture is old and sagging and draped in paisley and tie-dyed covers, and the scuffed and marred original hardwood floors are covered with brightly colored shag rugs, but in spite of the age and condition of its contents and the disrepair of the hurricane-ravaged home, everything is clean and relatively tidy.

"She always lived simply," Dad says. "Whether she had money or a man, she always chose a Spartan approach."

"Is that her?" I ask.

I point to the small framed photograph of a young girl with braided hair and a bikini top at what looks to be Woodstock. It's on a small bookshelf along the back wall in front of books on Eastern philosophy, meditation, feminism, the 60s, racism, social justice, home remedies, Eastern medicine, gardening, polyamory, free love, folk music, and Laurel Canyon. *The Electric Kool-Aid Acid Test, Fear and Loathing in Las Vegas,* and *The Rape of Nanking* are mixed in with pamphlets, printouts, and spiral bound booklets on peace, revolution, apocalypse, conspiracy-theory propaganda on the earth being flat, vaccinations causing autism and immune diseases, the moon landing being faked, UFOs, financial manipulation, corporate America, and the assassinations of MLK, JFK, and RFK.

He nods. "That's her. She was actually there." He frowns and shakes his head. "Think about all the experiences, memories, knowledge, and wisdom that cease to exist when someone like her dies."

"Hey," Reggie says, "look what I found."

We join her in the kitchen. On the counter is a paper bag with a bottle of champagne in it. The receipt inside shows Nell had purchased two identical bottles.

"She got them today," she says. "Not a lot of time for someone to sneak in here and poison them."

Dad says, "We need to get this bottle, the bag, and the receipt to FDLE for processing."

She nods. "I know she's a close friend of your family . . . but . . . we've got to consider every possibility. Could it have been suicide? She bought the champagne. She's the only one who knew she was going to do the little toast. She kept everything in her trunk. She's the only one who had access to it."

"It's certainly something we have to consider," I say. "She had far more access to everything than anyone else. And she may have been the only one with access to it."

"I have no problem considering it," Dad says, "but we've got to also consider the possibility that if she was poisoned, it wasn't from the champagne at all."

"That's true," she says. "It wasn't the first time, was it?"

THURSDAY, MAY 7, 2020

Thursday, May 7, 2020
1,245,728 confirmed cases and 69,700 deaths in the US

The World Health Organization issues a statement saying there is as yet no evidence that people who have recovered from COVID-19 and have antibodies are protected from a second infection.

In Georgia, gyms, tattoo parlors, hair and nail salons, massage therapists, and other businesses are allowed to reopen.

The CDC cautions that six new symptoms could be signs of the coronavirus—chills, repeated shaking with chills, muscle pain, headache, sore throat, and a loss of taste or smell.

Both government leaders and private industry experts warn of a possible meat shortage due to a breakdown in the food supply chain as coronavirus outbreaks in processing plants and factories spread throughout the country.

The US economy shrinks 4.8 percent in the first quarter of 2020—the first such shrinkage in output since early 2014, and the steepest decline since late 2008 during the depths of the Great Recession.

The US unemployment rate hits its highest since the Great Depression. The economy loses 20.5 million jobs in April and the unemployment rate rises to 14.7 percent.

46

D ays pass.
Then a few more.
Then a week.

Then another one.

Nell's small, sad funeral is limited to immediate family. The only exceptions are Jules, and Lavinia—and me to provide security.

The only comfort and consolation given is verbal, as social distancing is practiced.

"That may be the saddest thing I've ever seen," Lavinia says, tears still streaming from her red eyes.

"We'll give her a proper sendoff if we're still here once the pandemic is over," Jules says.

We are at Jules's home where Lavinia and Lillian are now living.

Though the tox tests aren't back yet, we believe she was murdered—poisoned with cyanide.

The ME explained that when cyanide is combined with hemoglobin in the blood—which is essentially how it kills, by blocking the utilization of oxygen within the cells—it creates a compound called cyanohemoglobin. The compound, which is bright red, turns the blood a cherry color that can also be seen more faintly in organs and tissue—and any lividity that might be present tends to be pinkish instead of the more typical blue-gray.

Not only did the ME observe red and pink evidence in the body, but he ruled out carbon monoxide, which can sometimes show a similar cherrying of the blood, tissue, and organs.

He had also been able to detect the faint odor of burnt almonds during the autopsy—yet another sign of cyanide poisoning. He explained that only about half of the population are genetically able to detect that particular smell, and he happened to fall within that group.

"And poor Jasmine . . ." Lavinia says. "Honestly didn't know she had that kind of grief in her. She's always been flighty and . . ."

"Aloof?" Jules offers.

"Yes, aloof."

"She's actually the reason we wanted to talk to you, John," Jules says. "There's something we need to tell you. Something we just found out. We—well, *I*, want to start by saying I don't suspect Jasmine."

"It's not that I suspect her," Lavinia says. "I just don't share your absolute certainty that she had nothing to do with it."

"Right, anyway . . ." Jules says. "As you probably know . . . Carson didn't leave Nell a pot to piss in or a window to throw it out of when he left her. She's been too poor to paint and too proud to whitewash ever since. Lavinia and I have been helping her get by these past few years, but we've had to do it like a preacher sneakin' out of a whorehouse."

"I ain't rich as Croesus myself," Lavinia says. "Nothing like Jules, but if I had known how bad things had really gotten for Nell, I would've tried to do more."

Jules says, "Poor dear had defaulted on just about everything, was up to her saggin' tits in debt, but there was one thing she never missed a payment on, was never even a moment late on. Lots of times she acted like she didn't have good walking-around sense—like her brain bounced around in her head like a BB in a boxcar, but . . . somehow she managed to take care of this."

"Life insurance?" I ask.

Jules nods.

"How'd you know?" Lavinia asks.

"What else would y'all feel the need to talk to the person investigating her death about?" I say. "And since y'all started by saying you don't suspect Jasmine . . . I take it she's the beneficiary."

They nod.

"How much?" I ask.

"We hear north of a quarter million," Jules says.

"Which isn't an obscene or unreasonable amount," Lavinia says, "but Jasmine manages her money like her mama did. So not only does she have none, but she's got a lot of debt too. Nell left her nothing—no inheritance to speak of. No home. No land. No heirlooms. But the money from the insurance policy will get her out of the fix she's in and put some folding money in her pocket."

"We knew it was going to come out eventually," Jules says. "We wanted you to hear it from us and *I* wanted to say that there's no way Jasmine would kill her mama for money."

"And I probably would've agreed with that before Paul came back into the picture," Lavinia says. "But now I'm just not sure. He's against everything she stands for—and she stays with him. He treats her sons like shit—even his own boy—and she stays with him. He can talk her into anything. And I'm not even sayin' he got her to do it. He could've done it."

"Now that's something we finally agree on," Jules says.

"Well, see if you can also agree with me on this . . ." Lavinia says. "I am not—under any circumstances—having a birthday party."

"We can agree," Jules says. "'Cause I wouldn't come if you did."

"I'd just as soon go on to sleep and y'all wake me up when it's next year," Lavinia says. "Between the hurricane and the pandemic and Nellie Bell and someone trying to kill us . . . makes me wish I had forwarded all those messages on Facebook."

47

———

"What is wrong with people?" Dad asks.

Though his question is obviously rhetorical, I answer it anyway.

"So very many things," I say, "but the particular malady that leads to this kind of inhumanity is largely fear."

We are standing in front of Red Star Chinese Garden, the little Chinese Restaurant in Pottersville, looking at the hateful message the vandals had scrawled across it in red spray paint.

It reads Take Your Kung Flu and Go Home.

"They've been closed for weeks," Dad says. "And now this."

During the COVID-19 pandemic most restaurants have remained open, with masked staff delivering takeout orders to vehicles in parking lots. But because of sentiments like the one painted across the front of their building and a rumor around town that customers were catching the virus from eating here, the Red Star has been closed almost from the very beginning of the crisis.

The fear and ignorance and hatred makes me livid, but I'm curious why Dad's called me out of my jurisdiction and into his county to show it to me.

"Any idea who did it?" I ask.

He nods and points to the security cameras at the corners of the building. "Pretty good idea."

I wait.

"Deputy just picked him up," he says. "They're on the way up here now. Feel bad for him with his grandmother just dying and all, but . . ."

"Nash?" I ask.

He nods.

I frown and shake my head and blink my stinging eyes.

"I'm gonna turn him over to you," he says. "Let you deal with it instead of the legal system."

"Thank you," I say. "I really appreciate it."

"Just save him," he says. "The last thing we need in this town and in the world is another bigot."

NASH IS quiet as we drive to the hardware store to buy the paint remover and brushes, but begins to talk some as we scrub his hateful words from the face of the little building.

I've yet to ask him any questions or initiate any conversation, so anything he offers is of his own volition.

As we work together to remove the paint, applying the various chemical compounds we picked up, scrubbing the spray paint marks, then washing it off with industrial soap and water, his voice changes, and as I glance at him I see his eyes are moist.

"I'm sorry," he says. "Sorry I was stupid enough to do this lame ass shit. Sorry you have to help me. Sorry people are looking at us. Sorry I'm keeping you away from looking for my grandmother's killer."

"It's not really me you owe the apology to, is it?"

"No."

"And I wouldn't even worry about people looking when you're doing the right thing—even when it's to fix a wrong one."

"I just meant . . . you're a cop and a minister, a good person. I'm sure you're embarrassed to be doing this."

"I'm ashamed of and embarrassed by what it says," I say, "not by being seen helping you clean it off."

"I didn't . . . even . . . I'm not sure what it even means. Alex just bet Kemp I was too chicken shit to do it . . . and . . . Madison was standing there."

"You did it to impress a girl?" I say.

He frowns and nods. "Yeah."

"You sure you want to impress a girl who can be impressed by something like this?"

He shakes his head. "No, guess not. I . . . I don't know what's wrong with me. I wasn't thinking. Didn't even . . . I just did it—like the moment Alex mentioned it I was like, 'Where's some spray paint?' I was . . . I was so glad they had stopped talkin' about how nuts my mom is for a minute. Kemp was like, 'Home School's too big of a pussy to do something that takes that much balls' . . . and Madison kinda snickered . . . and . . ."

"They call you Home School?"

"Yeah. Some other things too, but that's my main nickname."

Since he doesn't attend school—his mom has always condemned the curriculum as imperialist, racist, sexist bullshit designed to kill creativity and originality, refused to subject him to the shots required, and claimed she is a better teacher anyway—I wonder where he's encountering Alex, Kemp, and Madison.

I start to ask him, but Mr. Li, the owner of the restaurant, pulls up.

As he approaches us, walking quickly and deliberately, Nash turns toward him, his body tensing, but doesn't raise his hands in self-defense.

I angle my body slightly so I can protect Nash if Li decides to do anything to him, but instead of attacking, he bends down, picks up the supplies, and begins helping us remove the spray paint.

Nash and I return to the paint removal, and though he never stops scrubbing, he begins sobbing and apologizing profusely to Mr. Li.

And as tears sting my own eyes, I know that Nash is going to be okay.

48

As we pull up to Jasmine's place, T-Rex and Graham are pulling away.

Jasmine is in the front yard, Harley on her hip, tears in her eyes, an expression of fear and confusion on her face.

Nash and I climb out of my truck and he rushes over to her.

"What's wrong, Mom?" he asks.

"Don't act like you care," she says. "All I'm dealin' with and you pull a stunt like that."

"I'm—"

"I don't want to hear a single word out of you," she says. "Do you understand me? Carried away in a police car from my house . . . Defacing property . . . Spreading fear and hate . . . Attacking a small, vulnerable minority community . . . NO. Not a word. And just wait until Paul gets a hold of you. He's gonna tan your hide and I'm gonna help him."

My plan had been to drop him off and talk to Jasmine about the life insurance, but hearing her threaten him with Paul, seeing the fear in his face as she did . . .

"I've been dealing with him about it all afternoon," I say.

"And Dad said if I'd be the one to handle it, he wouldn't be arrested or have any kind of record. Is it okay with you if he stays with me tonight so I can keep dealing with it?"

She hesitates.

"If you'd rather it be handled in the courts I can call—"

"No, no, that's fine. Take him. I can't deal with all this right now anyway." She hands Harley to him. "Take your brother and go pack a bag. Let me talk to John a minute."

He does as he's told, risking her wrath to say a soft, "I'm sorry, Mama," as he walks away.

"So, T-Rex was just here," she says after Nash and Harley are gone.

"I saw him pulling away."

"He said Mom owed him money when she died," she says. "That's not all that surprising. She owed everyone, but . . . He said that her debt is my debt now, that I owe him what she owed him, plus interest that's accruing every day. I still can't believe she's really gone, and now this. It's making me crazy. I miss her and I'm mad at her and I love her and I hate her all at the same time."

The front door of the house opens and she spins around and yells, "I thought I told you—"

She stops when she sees it's Paul.

"Oh," she says, "sorry. I thought you were the boys."

"Tell her she's overreacting," he says to me.

"*Overreacting*?" she says. "My mother was *murdered*."

"I wasn't talking about that, but . . . she was old and . . . you're acting as if a young person was tragically struck down. She had a good, long life. But no, I was talking about what Nash did. Come on, it was funny. Kung Flu."

She shakes her head. "Anyway," she says to me, "the most surprising thing he said was Mom had a life insurance policy and the first thing I better pay out of it is what she owes him.

How can a short-armed drug-dealing moron know my mom had life insurance when I don't?"

"You knew," Paul says.

"No, I didn't."

"You did. You had to. I knew. Everybody did. She'd always say she might lose everything else, but she'd never stop paying on it so she could leave you an inheritance. Like she was trying to make up for your childhood or something."

"She never said anything like that to me," she says.

"Well, I know I heard her say it," he says. "And more than once."

"T-Rex says it's the only reason he gave her credit and that he has a signed IOU from her and that one way or another he's going to collect. He even intimated that the reason she's dead is so her debts can be paid."

MONDAY, MAY 11, 2020

Monday, May 11, 2020
1,338,720 confirmed cases and 74,735 deaths in the US

More than fifteen states are set to move forward with reopening procedures. Shops and schools reopen across Germany and France, while British Prime Minister Boris Johnson "actively encourages" people who can't work from home to return to their jobs.

"It is so transmissible, and it is so widespread throughout the world, that even if our infections get well controlled and go down dramatically during the summer, there is virtually no chance it will be eradicated," Dr. Fauci says. "Now, even if the virus goes down dramatically in June and July and August, as the virus starts returning in the fall, it would be, in my mind, shame on us if we don't have in place all of the mechanisms to prevent it from blowing up again."

49

"Okay," Reggie is saying, "so I thought it'd be helpful for us all to get together and discuss our investigations—talk about what we know so far, share what we're thinking and doing, and coordinate our activities."

We are in the conference room of our new building in Port St. Joe, each sitting about six feet apart from one another.

Reggie and I are here representing Gulf County. Dad and Gerald Woodson are present for Potter County. And Pine County is being represented by a sheriff's investigator named Neil Byrd.

Coffee, doughnuts, and assorted pastries are on a side table, but so far only Dad has availed himself of any of it—and that was just black coffee.

"I'm sure the quarantine and need for social distancing is hindering your investigations as much as ours, so I thought we might share any strategies or best practices as far as that goes too," Reggie says. "Telephonic or even video conferencing interviews are so much more challenging and less effective than in-person interviews."

A few of us nod, but nobody says anything so she moves on.

"Okay, well, if you think of anything you want to share before we wrap up, feel free. Why don't I start with what we have. Toxicology results are back and confirm what the ME suspected. Nell Harbuck was poisoned with cyanide. Since the ME was fairly certain that was the case, we've already been treating her death as a homicide, but now that we have confirmation we can . . . It helps knowing for sure."

She looks at me.

"We still have far more questions than answers," I say. "We don't even have our *why* yet. The only possible motive we've uncovered so far is a possible money one for the family, but her daughter, Jasmine Carter, claims not to have known about the $250,000 life insurance policy that she's the beneficiary of. Her boyfriend, Paul Branch, admits to knowing about it and says Jasmine did too. Jasmine says that Nell owed her supplier, Timothy T-Rex Hitt, who has indicated he knew about the policy and expects to be paid out of it and may have intimated that's why Nell was killed."

I pause but no one says anything. Since our department, like all county agencies, is closed to the public, and only essential personnel are present in the building, outside the conference room is as still and quiet as if we're here on a Sunday morning in December.

"We haven't uncovered any other motives yet—unless we go back to the poisoning that took place at Jules Jordan's party on March 14th and expand possible motives to the two other poisoning victims from that night—Jules Jordan and Lavinia Pritchett—which I'm sure the esteemed sheriff of Gulf County will address, but all that does is raise more questions. Were all three women the intended targets or was it just Nell all along? If only Nell, why poison all three at Jules's party? Was it an accident? Were the other two poisoned to obfuscate the real intended victim? Or are Jules and Lavinia still in danger? Did the killer try to kill Jules at Nell's party and fail, or just didn't have the opportunity? Was the plan to kill each of them at their own birthday parties all along? If so, will the killer now improvise? Are their birthdays significant or just a place of opportunity? If the latter, who in their life only has access to them at their parties?"

This time when I pause, Reggie moves us to the next subject.

"Beyond the *why,* which we don't know," she says, "there's the *how.* We know that the first poison was introduced into the honey each woman took prior to performing, but we don't know how the killer was able to get into the dressing room and put the poison into the honey."

"How he or she even knew the honey was there to put the poison in," I add.

"Exactly," she says. "And in the case of Nell's poisoning . . . we know she shared a secret champagne toast with a few close friends prior to the official one with everybody, but we don't know for sure that's how she was poisoned. It's the still the best possibility, but the lab found no traces of cyanide in the glasses or the bottle."

"The fact that no trace of the poison was found doesn't necessarily mean that's not how she was poisoned," I say, "but it does mean we need to keep searching to see if we can find any other substances she ingested or came in contact with. If it was in her champagne, we've got to figure out how the killer knew which glass Nell would use. How did he or she introduce the poison into that glass? Nell brought the champagne and glasses from home and kept them locked in her car—something no one seems to have known about."

"The autopsy revealed no puncture wounds or any other signs to indicate Nell was poisoned in any other manner than by something she ingested," Reggie says.

"Remember," I say, "cyanide is very dangerous and represented a real risk for the killer. He or she would've had to have been very careful."

"This case . . ." Woodson says.

"Most baffling shit I've never encountered," Neil Byrd says.

"But the question isn't only how and what the killer got the poison into, but was it what he or she meant to do. As in the case of the glass—was it the right glass? Was it really meant for Nell? And if so, why not poison Jules who is right there too? And Lillian, who he had possibly tried to attack at her home the week before? Of course that raises the question why try to attack Lillian at all? And why in such a different manner? Is it unrelated to the poisonings? Or does the killer intend to kill not only the Tupelo Queens but their offspring as well? And speaking of differing methods . . . why use two different poisons? Why use oxycodone the first time and cyanide the second? Cyanide is much more dangerous to deal with, so he took a much bigger risk the second time. Why? And the oxy he used the first time came from the residence—it was for Jules's husband who had recently passed away—but there's no sign that there was any cyanide at the Harrison house. Why? Was the first attempt unplanned? Did he decide at the party to do it and just went in search of what was available? Did he or she know it was there the way he knew the honey was—and that they took honey before every performance? Or is the killer manipulating things to look like other than what they really are?"

"How hard is it to get cyanide?" Neil Byrd asks.

"Not hard at all," I say. "It's used in jewelry making and metal plating and is readily available at chemical supply houses. It can also be ordered online in the form of sodium cyanide or potassium cyanide."

"I hate to sound like an ignorant hick," Byrd says, "but that's what I am. I've never seen anything like this and all of this is way above my pay grade, but . . ." He glances at Reggie. "And please don't take offense at this, but . . . isn't poison a woman's weapon?"

"Nothing offensive about that," she says. "And you're right, it has been known historically as a woman's weapon. Probably not quite as true as it once was, but . . . I bet if we check the statistics, women still use poison far more than men."

"Thanks," he says. "Is it at least possible that all three cases —the first and second poisonings and the attempted B and E out our way—aren't related at all?"

Reggie nods.

"Absolutely," I say. "It's certainly possible and something we have to consider."

He nods. "Okay. Well . . . you started by saying we have more questions than answers, but I'd say we only have questions."

50

———

"How many jobs you ever done that you didn't get paid for?" T-Rex asks.

Merrill says, "Including this one?"

Merrill and I track down T-Rex and Graham Arnold at the TL James sports complex, sitting on aluminum bleachers near the back softball field as if at a game—though they are the only two people in the entire complex, or were until we walked up on them.

They are eating Dixie Dandy pizza and drinking the champagne of beers from glass bottles—men of leisure, with nothing to do, nowhere to be.

It's late evening, and beneath the golden glow of the vanishing sun the dusty ballpark, like much of the rest of the planet, seems a relic of an earlier civilization in a now abandoned world.

"And just to be clear," T-Rex says. "I ain't afraid of you, Merrill."

"But you are of him?" Merrill asks, gesturing toward me.

He laughs and when he does Graham, as if T-Rex's personal laugh track, takes it as his cue to laugh too.

"Nobody's scared of *him*," T-Rex says.

"Yeah," Graham says, "nobody's scared of him."

"No offense, John," T-Rex says, "but everybody knows behind that badge you're a preacher or a social worker or some shit like that. Hard to be a tough guy while trying to breastfeed everybody."

"None taken," I say with a smile.

"That's a relief," he says. "Wouldn't'a slept a wink tonight if I thought I'd hurt your feelings." He looks back at Merrill. "I know there's plenty a people scared of you. I just ain't one of 'em."

T-Rex is a good deal more intelligent than he let on when I spoke to him at the party.

"What I care if you're scared of me or not?" Merrill says.

"Well, I'll tell you," he says. "If you threaten me to stay away from Bell's daughter and not try to collect my money . . ."

Evidently, he was close enough with her to drop the Nellie and just call her Bell.

". . . I'd need to feel threatened in order to actually stay away from her and write off what she owes me, now wouldn't I?"

"She doesn't owe you anything," I say.

"'Course she does," he says. "In my business all debt is transferable. And it transferred to her. And not just her, but that boy of hers you seem so fond of. What is it with you fuckin' priests and little boys?"

I take a step toward him.

"Social distancing," he says. "Social distancing. Back the fuck up."

"Think it time we skip ahead to the threats," Merrill says.

"Go ahead," he says. "I got some too."

"Oh, well you go first then."

"I know y'all are carrying," he says. "But I am too. Plus I got this big bastard right here." He jerks his head toward Graham. He's got retard strength. So if y'all want to tussle . . . I like our chances. So . . . make your threats or not . . . won't change a thing. Or we can get straight to fisticuffs or a shootout and see what happens."

"Your kind's already been extinct once," Merrill says. "Didn't teach you anything, did it?"

"Or," he says, as if Merrill hasn't spoken, "you can cuff me and take me in, but—"

"*Cuff you*?" Merrill says. "Bitch, your baby dinosaur arms aren't long enough to cuff in the front or the back."

T-Rex is a drug dealer and very likely a murderer, but Merrill's attack on a physical disability that is out of his control hurts my heart—especially when imagining him as a kid being made fun of by the other kids.

"Okay," T-Rex says, "so at least we've ruled out one of the options."

"How much did Nell owe you when she died?" I ask.

"Three stacks," he says.

"*What*?" Merrill says. "You really are smalltime, aren't you? All this over three Gs."

"I have IOUs from her with her signature on them," he says. "I'm a legit businessman. Straight up. Never cheated anybody out of a dime. I can't be scared or threatened. I won't be cheated and I don't cheat anyone."

"Your word if I pay you what she owed you, that'll be the end of it," I say.

"My word," he says, nodding and smiling, unable to conceal his pleasure.

"Better be," Merrill says. "Only other option is one of my bullets in your tiny lizard brain."

When we're back in the truck, Merrill says, "Couldn't do that if I was wearing a badge too. Tell your dad I appreciate the offer—more than he knows—but I think I can do more good staying private."

THURSDAY, MAY 14, 2020

Thursday, May 14, 2020

1,407,517 confirmed cases and 79,899 deaths in the US

The US has conducted more than 10.2 million coronavirus tests, with approximately 15 percent of people testing positive.

The CDC releases six one-page checklists providing guidance to schools, businesses, restaurants and more on when and how to safely reopen.

Deaths worldwide pass three hundred thousand—eighty-five thousand of those in the US.

President Trump announces Operation Warp Speed, a government coordinating effort aimed at securing a coronavirus vaccine by the end of the year.

51

___

"She's been through enough," Lavinia says. "I want her left out of this."

"She asked to speak with me," I say.

I'm driving back toward town after dropping Merrill off at his car.

Earlier I had received a message from Lillian that she needed to talk to me about information she has that might be relevant to Nell's case, but before I can call her back, Lavinia calls me.

"I know," she says, "and she has some information that might be beneficial, but I want your word that you'll leave her out of it. I don't want that disgusting man knowing this came from her."

"Which disgusting man?" I ask.

"Will you leave her out of it?"

"If I can."

"That's not good enough. She's so fragile right now. You can't imagine how this has made her feel. She thinks she killed her own child. And I know she's thought about . . . about actually harming . . . herself, so give me your word, John."

"You have my word that the disgusting man won't know the information came from her," I say.

"She's at the cemetery," she says. "And don't just get the information you need, see if you can help her some too."

Lillian sits on the stone bench beneath the southern magnolia tree facing the small grave with the marble headstone and the too, too short lifespan represented by the tiny dash between the birth and death dates etched into it.

I slowly approach and ease down on the bench beside her, the sweet fragrance of magnolia blossoms filling my nostrils.

We sit for a long time in silence.

I can feel the grief emanating from her like heat waves off August asphalt. I can also feel myself absorbing them.

Eventually, she says, "I know I should be over this by now."

I shake my head. "This isn't something you get over."

"It isn't, is it?"

"Give yourself permission to grieve for as long and as intensely as you need to," I say. "And when you feel like grieving less or in a different way or doing other things besides, give yourself permission to do that without guilt as well."

"I just can't get over how this has hit me," she says. "I know people are saying 'you barely met her, how can you be so broken up about someone you barely knew?'"

"Length of time relating has little to do with grief, and at least part of what you're experiencing is the great loss of all the possibilities, all the paths now not traveled, all she would have become."

"Exactly," she says. "That's exactly it."

We are quiet a moment, and I think of how much I grieved when I lost Martin Fisher or when John Paul didn't become my son after I thought he was going to.

"Thank you," she says. "You're always so kind and understanding with me. So patient. I really appreciate it, but I'm not gonna take up any more of your time. The reason I asked to talk to you is because of something I saw at the party."

"Don't feel pressured to talk about that yet if you're not ready," I say. "You don't have to say anything. Or you can talk about Lilliana more."

"Thank you for saying her name. That means a lot. I'm fine to talk about it. I really am. It's probably nothing, but I've heard y'all still don't know how Aunt Nell got the poison. Is that true?"

"It is," I say.

"So it wasn't in the champagne?"

"There were no traces found in the bottle or the six glasses, but that's still our leading theory of how she ingested it because we don't know of anything else she ate or drank."

"Well, I know of something," she says. "Not sure if it counts or not, but I thought I better tell you. After her little stunt with the toast at the car, we headed back toward the party. We were sort of spread out—Charles and Jules were putting everything in the trunk and everybody walks at different speeds and we tried to practice a little social distancing. Anyway . . . Aunt Nell and I were together. I don't think anyone else was really around —not very close at any rate. As we turned at the edge of the driveway at the front corner of the house, the dealer they call T-Rex passed by and handed Aunt Nell a vape pen and she took a few hits on it as we walked the rest of the way. I have no idea if the poison could've been given to her that way, but . . . I thought you should know."

"That's extremely helpful," I say. "Thank you very much."

She stands. I join her. As we begin ambling toward our vehicles, I let her dictate the pace.

"I come here every day," she says. "This is the first day I feel better as I'm leaving."

"Don't hesitate to call if you need to talk," I say. "I'm happy to listen to anything you ever need to express. And if you ever want to speak to a counselor who specializes in grief, I'd be happy to arrange it."

"Thank you," she says. "I might just— Wait. You said *six*."

"I said what?"

"Six," she says. "You said *six*, but there were *seven* champagne glasses. I was standing by the trunk. I could see. After Nell passed out the glasses to everyone, there was still one left in the trunk. There were seven."

52

"**I** may have made a deal to pay the murderer," I say.

"Well, if you did," Anna says, "you'll just arrest him instead."

It's dim and quiet, our whispered words and breathing the only sounds in the room. We are in the larger of the two upstairs bedrooms—the one mostly used as a playroom for the girls. Nash is across the landing in what has now become his bedroom. The girls are asleep downstairs in their room.

Since shortly after the COVID-19 pandemic began, this has been my bedroom. We decided back then that since I was going to be out in the world working in such close proximity with so many people, that I would maintain a certain social distancing and self-quarantining at home. This would not only help protect Anna and the girls, but also keep her healthy in case she needed to care for her parents or Dad and Verna.

Being separated from them in this way, isolated in my own home, has been far, far more painful and difficult that I had imagined it would be—and I imagined it would be absolute hell.

"Of course, he could've had nothing to do with it," I say,

"and it all comes down to the missing glass. I still don't see how I missed that."

"How were you to know that there was an extra glass?" she says.

"I should've asked," I say. "I know better than to make assumptions. Well, evidently I don't, but I should."

"But six is a set," she says. "Like four or eight or ten or even two, but not seven."

"I should've remembered that she said she wanted Jasmine to join her but couldn't locate her. I should've realized then that there would be an extra glass."

"So what do you think happened to it?" she asks.

"It could still be in the trunk," I say. "Could've slipped down into the spare tire well. It could've been lost by the crime scene techs or the lab. But if I had to bet, I'd say the killer removed it."

"How?"

"The two most obvious ways are either he or she had a key and went back into the trunk after everyone had left—or during the confusion and pandemonium after Nell died. Or . . . took it with him or her after the toast. It'd be easy to do. No one was concerned about the bottle or glasses or anything after the toast. The killer could've been in the small group and could've pretended to be helping collect everything. He or she could have taken it from Nell and turned as if to give it to Aunt Jules or Charles Harbuck and just handed them his. That wouldn't've stood out to them in the least. They would've only expected him or her to hand them one anyway. It was dark and all done very quickly. Would've been easy to do—just slip it in a pocket or in a sleeve—if he or she were certain the cyanide had been removed. Very dangerous otherwise."

"So the murderer could've been in that small group of the people she loved and trusted the most?"

"Before we go too far down that path," I say, "I need to

check the trunk of Nell's car to make sure the glass is not still inside. Excuse me, just a second."

I pull out my phone and call Reggie and ask her where the car is and if I can check the trunk later tonight or first thing in the morning.

I'm surprised when she says no. I'm shocked when she explains why.

"Nell's daughter Jasmine picked it up yesterday," she says.

"How'd she do that?" I say. "I still have the key."

"Evidently, she has a spare," Reggie says.

"Which means . . ." I say, "that the person with the single biggest motive could've gotten into the trunk to poison her glass and or gotten back in afterwards to destroy the evidence."

"Lower you voice," Anna says, "you wouldn't want your little buddy across the way to hear you accusing his mother of murder."

"Think we need to conduct another official interview with her in the morning," Reggie says.

"I agree," I say a bit more quietly, "but let's do it at the station so Nash doesn't see."

"Okay," she says, "but you know, John, sometimes your good deeds are a fuckin' conflict of interest for you."

By the time I'm off the call, Anna has disrobed and stands naked before me.

The faint moonlight streaming through the window bathes her body in a pale muted glow, accentuating her curves and the soft suppleness of her flesh.

I've missed her—all of her—so much, and I hunger for her with an existential ache.

"You're so beautiful," I whisper.

"Take your clothes off," she says. "I'd love to but I can't from six feet away."

We haven't kissed or caressed or held each other or made love since I started self-quarantining. Everything we've done, both verbally and sexually, has been from at least six feet apart.

"So," she says, "the more the experts learn, the more they believe transmission is from face-to-face contact—especially when someone is talking, singing, or yelling. I know how protective you are of me and the girls and I appreciate it more than you can ever know, but this, us making love, is an acceptable risk—and well, well worth it. Well worth it. So this is what we're going to do. I'm going to lie facedown on the bed and you're going to make love to me from behind without a word—no talking, singing, or yelling."

"I'm not sure I can do it without singing," I say.

She laughs. "Do your best. I'm going to keep my head down. You keep yours up. Singing isn't the only urge you're going to have to resist. As much as you'll want to, don't pull my hair. And as much as I'm gonna want to turn my head back and kiss you, I'm going to resist that urge."

We make love in the manner she prescribed, and it was the perfect meal after a long fast.

Later, long after she is gone, long after I've exhausted my mind thinking about the case, I drift to sleep and have my recurring dream about my son.

The last of the setting sun streaks the blue horizon with neon pink and splatters the emerald green waters of the Gulf with giant orange splotches like scoops of sherbet in an Art Deco bowl.

A fitting finale for a perfect Florida day.

My son, who looks to be around four, though it's hard to tell since in dreams we all seem ageless—runs up from the water's edge, his face red with sun and heat, his hands sticky with wet sand, and asks me to join him for one last swim.

He looks up at me with his mother's brown eyes, open and honest as possible, and smiles his sweetest smile as he begins to beg.

"Please, Daddy," he says. "Please."

"We need to go," I say. "It'll be dark soon. And I'm supposed to take your mom out on a date tonight."

"Please, Daddy," he repeats as if I have not spoken, and now he takes the edge of my swimming trunks in his tiny, sandy hand and tugs.

I look down at him, moved by his openness, purity, and beauty.

He knows he's got me then.

"Yes," he says, releasing my shorts to clench his fist and pull it toward him in a gesture of victory. Then he begins to jump up and down.

I drop the keys and the towels and the bottles of sunscreen wrapped in them, kick off my flip-flops, and pause just a moment to take it all in—him, the sand, the sea, the sun.

"I love you, Dad," he says with the ease and unashamed openness only a safe and secure child can.

"I love you."

I take his hand in mine, and we walk down to the end of his world as the sun sets and the breeze cools off the day. And we walk right into the ocean from which we came. A wave knocks us down and we stay that way, allowing the foamy water to wash over us.

He shrieks his joy and excitement, sounding like the gulls in the air and on the shore. He plays with intensity and abandon, and for a moment I want to be a child again, but only for a moment, for more than anything in this world, I want to be his dad.

We forget about the world around us, and we lose track of time, and the thick, salty waters of the Gulf roll in on us and then back out to sea.

53

———

We're not able to interview Jasmine Carter.

When Reggie and I arrive at her home, we find EMTs attempting unsuccessfully to revive her.

After they have gone and we're awaiting the arrival of the FDLE crime scene unit and an investigator from the ME's office, we interview Paul Branch.

"Tell us what happened," Reggie says.

Nash is still asleep at our house. I text Anna and tell her what has happened and ask her to take his phone. After leaving here I will have to go tell him that his mother is dead.

Harley is with Lillian, Lavinia, and Jules at her place. I had asked them to come pick him up when we arrived and saw what was happening.

"I don't know," Paul is saying. "I woke up and went to pee and found her on the floor in the bathroom like that. I could tell she wasn't asleep. Knew something was wrong. Her—well, *one* of her pill bottles was on the floor not far from her and most of the pills had spilled out. She must've gotten up in the middle of the night to take something and . . ."

"You didn't hear her?" Reggie asks.

"I'm a sound sleeper," he says.

"Was she fine when she went to bed? What time was that?"

He shrugs. "Don't know. She was a night owl. Always came to bed after me."

"So you don't even know if she came to bed?" I say.

"She was in bed the first time I got up to pee," he says.

"And she was alive?"

"Snoring like an old diesel engine."

"What time did you go to bed?" I ask.

He shrugs. "Ten, maybe."

"Did she often get up to take meds in the middle of the night?" Reggie asks.

"She often took meds," he says. "Day. Night. Early. Late. Anti-anxiety, anti-depression, diet pills. You name it, she took it."

"I understand that was a recent occurrence," I say.

"Yeah, I guess. But she took to it."

"Had she complained about or mentioned or shown any signs of any unusual symptoms lately?" Reggie asks.

"No. Nothing."

"Had she gotten any drugs recently?" she says. "Prescription or otherwise, from a pharmacist or otherwise."

"She only took prescription drugs as far as I know," he says. "Why wouldn't she? She would get what she wanted and her insurance paid for most of it. She didn't even do weed and never drank much. Just pills. Nothing new lately. She stocked up when this pandemic shit first kicked off—not that she needed to, she already had enough to open her own drugstore chain, but nothing since then and nobody's given her anything that I've seen."

Reggie starts to say something, but he cuts her off.

"Y'all ain't said it right now, but I know what you're thinking. So let me be crystal clear. I didn't kill her. Didn't have anything to do with it. Don't know who did. On my life, as God is my witness. I know you gotta suspect me—as the boyfriend and beneficiary—but don't waste too much time doing that."

"Beneficiary of what?" Reggie asks.

"Her mom's money," he says. "It's— I just realized. She died before her mom's money has even arrived. That's nuts."

"So you're sayin' she had a will that names you as—"

"Well, no, but—"

"And y'all weren't married?"

"Hell no."

"Did she have life insurance?"

"No."

"So how is it you think you're her beneficiary?" Reggie says.

"I was her boyfriend," he says. "The father of her son."

54

———

When I tell Nash his mom has died, I shed more tears than he does.

It's not that he doesn't emote. He does. But it's subdued and only involves a few tears.

I am shattered inside for the broken boy beside me. I can feel pieces of my emotional core shifting, particles breaking apart, flying away. In addition to mourning for and with him and the loss of his mom, part of me mourns for my mom and my loss of her.

The two of us are in his room, sitting on the edge of the bed. Anna and the girls are in the front yard to give us quiet and privacy.

"What happened?" he says.

His voice is soft and sad, his words coming out slowly, weakly, as if each one barely makes it out and will be the last to do so.

I tell him a little of the little we know.

"Was she poisoned like Grandma Nell?" he asks.

"We just don't know yet," I say. "As soon as we do, I will let you know. First thing. I promise."

"But what do you think?" he asks.

"I think there's a good possibility, but . . . there's just no way to know for sure yet."

"Who would . . . want . . . to kill them?"

"I'm going to find out," I say. "I promise you that."

"Are we all in danger? Is Harley?"

"I'm not sure," I say, "but we're going to protect you guys like you are."

I think about my own mother again, about my conflicted relationship with her, about losing her. In so many ways I was younger than Nash is now when I lost her to the slow suicide and living death of addiction.

"What's going to happen to me?" he asks.

His voice is the smallest, softest, most pitiful, most little boy like that it has thus far been.

"We'll figure that out together," I say. "I will take care of you. I'm not going anywhere. Ever. You can count on that. Do you know that?"

He nods.

I say, "I will make sure you're okay, no matter what."

"I don't want to live with Paul," he says. "Not that he'd want me, but—"

"You absolutely do not have to live with Paul," I say. "Not for another second. You never have to see him again if you don't want to."

"I don't. But what about Harley?" he says. "He's . . . I mean he's part Paul's. What will happen to him?"

"We'll figure that out too," I say. "Do all we can to make sure he's okay. He won't just be dependent on Paul. We will all help. You know your grandmother's friends, Jules and Lavinia, will help. So will Lillian. They already are. They're taking good care of him now and will continue to."

"Doesn't seem real that she's really dead," he says. "Grandma Nell either. It's like my mind won't let me believe it."

"Nothing wrong with that right now," I say.

"But I know they are," he says. "I know I will never see my mama again. Never get to talk to her—tell her about my day. Never have her give me a hug and tell me everything's gonna be okay—because it's not. It's never going to be all okay ever again."

55

"He's doing great," Jules says about Harley. "And having him here is doing wonders for Lillian. I've never quite seen anything like it. I ain't sayin' she's happy as a jackass eatin' briars or anything, but her mood's at least cleared up to fair to partly cloudy—and it's been a coon's age since it's done that."

"That's great," I say. "Thanks again for taking him."

"Thank you," she says. "Despite the horrible tragedy, this is by far the best thing that's happened to us in a very, very long time."

I think about all she's been through with the hurricane and the death of her husband and the pandemic and the death of her friend and now her friend's daughter.

"Paul hasn't called or come by or anything," Jules says. "I know he's dealing with a lot, losing his girlfriend and all, but his son just lost his mother and he doesn't even check on him."

"Can't say I'm surprised," I say, "from what I've observed of him over the past year or so."

"He's a selfish, self-centered little prick and I wouldn't be surprised if he's behind all of this," she says. "Kill Nell for the life insurance. Kill Jasmine because she figured it out or even helped him or to get his hands on the money or just because that was his plan all along."

"He certainly indicated he thought he was going to get Nell's life insurance money."

"I can see it," she says. "It's so funny—I called to tell you something about another suspect and now I'm totally convinced it's Paul."

"Well, tell me about the other one anyway," I say.

"Oh, I will," she says. "Always up for spreadin' a little juicy gossip. But before we get to that, how is Nash doing? And how are you? You holdin' up okay through all this?"

I tell her.

"Good," she says. "Glad to hear it. Okay, so here it goes. Remember how I told you I was a bit of a detective?"

"I do," I say, "and I knew you were before you told me. I'm even aware of some of your exploits."

"I'm honored," she says. "Well, anyway, I've been having myself plenty of good thinks about everything and I've come up with something that might be nothing. But I'm telling you in case it's something."

"As opposed to nothing," I say.

"Exactly," she says. "The thing is . . . it's the birthdays."

"What is?"

"The connection," she says. "That's what made me think of it, anyway. If the killer was trying to kill each of us on our birthdays . . . and just made a mess of mine, then I may know the motive. And the murderer, of course."

"Lay it on me," I say.

"Well, back in the stone age when we were in school, one of us—I can't remember who, but it was probably your sassy ol' Aunt Jules—got into a little tiff with Dixie Ledoux and didn't go to her birthday party. I was a bit of a rounder back then and acted ugly sometimes. Ain't proud of it, but that was the lay of the land way back yonder. Thing is, not only did the three of us not go to her party, but we organized a little alternative concert party of our own, and nearly everyone ditched her party and came to ours. Not our finest moment, I assure you. We later kissed and made up—sort of. She said she let it go, but she never again invited us to her birthdays. Now, don't get ol' Jules wrong, I'm not saying she's doing it because of that, but if she is behind them, if she's nursed a grudge all these years and finally decided to take us off the board, then the icing on the cake would be doing it on our birthdays."

56

———

"What's that line about . . ." Dixie Ledoux is saying. "I don't know who said it, but it's something about . . . politicians, ugly buildings, and whores all get respectable if they last long enough. Something like that. I'm not calling the so-called Queens whores. That's not what I mean. I'm saying it's easy to forget how cruel and hateful and self-centered people were when they were young once they've gotten old."

We are speaking by phone because of the quarantine, which makes the follow-up interview even more challenging. I'm flying blind, unable to see any of her reactions, ticks, tells, or facial expressions. All I have to go on is her words and her manner of speaking—tone, intonation, emphasis.

"They were cruel to you?" I ask.

"I know you don't want to hear this about your aunt, but—"

"I want to hear anything and everything you have to say. Forget that she's my aunt. Don't hold back."

"'Course they were cruel. And not just in that popular-kids kind of way. Some of it was intentional and directed straight at me."

"I'm very sorry to hear that."

"You said you don't want me to hold back, well . . . I'd say . . . they deserve everything that befalls them. They're just reaping what they've sown for . . . decades. 'Do not be deceived my children. God is not mocked. For whatsoever a man sows, that shall he reap.'"

I nod encouragingly though she can't see me, and wait.

"Vengeance is up to God," she says. "Got nothing to do with me. I'm sure you suspect me. Hell, I would too if I was you, but I . . . haven't . . . tried to hurt anyone. Let alone killed them. And just remember, I didn't cater Nell's sad little birthday party."

"When you say 'tried' . . ." I say.

"Yeah?"

"Does that mean you may have done it without meaning to or—"

"I'm not saying—all I meant was, the Lord works in mysterious ways. I haven't knowingly done anything to the bitc—to them, but I don't really know what was done to them. So if someone poisoned something I served I could be involved without knowing it. And if that's the case it would be a sweet little revenge the Lord may have used me for, but I haven't tried to hurt or kill anyone. 'Vengeance is mine sayeth the Lord.' It's not for me to decide who and how divine justice is meted out."

"You're not sad Nell is dead?" I ask.

She makes a sound I can't quite make out. "Not particularly. She was the best of 'em, but silence is betrayal. Goin' along with others' cruelty is a type of cruelty itself. Remember those people who got convicted for cheering on someone who was raping that woman in the back of that bar that time?"

57

———

We find Donnie Ray Bryant the next day—though not the way we want to.

The victim of an apparent suicide, Lillian's ex and Lilliana's biological father is lying naked on top of a made bed in the guest room of his sister's beach house—one of the few not destroyed by Hurricane Michael.

The small, bright blue clapboard cottage on the Gulf side of Highway 98 in Port St. Joe Beach has been vacant since the pandemic had ended vacation rentals, and Donnie Ray's sister, Clarissa, had no idea he had been staying here. And, in fact, since he didn't have a key, he had broken in in order to do so.

"Why is he naked?" Reggie asks.

"It's a good question," I say. "It's significant—because it obviously has nothing to do with the manner of suicide. It's not as if he was engaged in autoerotic asphyxiation and accidentally killed himself."

"Thank Goddess," Reggie says. "Bad enough we have to see this."

"I've read a few interesting articles on the subject," I say. "The truth is there's a lot of speculation and not a lot of research, but some experts seem to associate nakedness in suicide to the verse from the book of Job in the Bible that says, 'Naked came I out of my mother's womb, and naked I shall return.'"

"That seems a stretch."

"I agree," I say, "though some of those things are far deeper in the culture than we know—especially among the mentally ill."

"And we know he was that," she says. "Little stalkin' bastard."

"Marilyn Monroe was found nude," I say. "And there's a famous painting of Cleopatra, who committed suicide after Mark Antony fell on his sword, naked on her death bed."

"Didn't she let herself get bitten by a poisonous snake or something?" Reggie asks.

"Seems like that's one of the legends," I say. "I'm not really sure."

"Some psychologists have suggested that the shedding of clothes may symbolize some kind of new beginning, a rebirth —a sloughing off of the old skin of the world. Some think it's meant to inflict trauma onto whoever finds the victim or sees him."

"It's certainly traumatizing," she says. "I feel for his poor sister."

"One doctor I read said that those who are severely depressed may get naked to commit suicide as a way of expressing their vulnerability, despair, desolation, and worth-lessness. Another said that if the victim is psychotic, being naked may be related to a delusion or auditory hallucinations —and a final self-abasement."

"Which is he?" she asks, jerking her head toward Donnie Ray.

I shrug. "No idea. We don't even know if it is suicide."

"True," she says, "but we've got a note—and the sister says

it's his handwriting. And he seems to be apologizing for not just the attack on her but the other poisonings and death."

Next to the body on the bed, in an unsteady hand on the back of an old, previously used envelope in blue ink is a note that reads: *Lilly, I'm sorry for attacking you and scaring you and what I've done to your grandma and her friends. I tried to love you but you wouldn't let me. I can't live with what I've done and without you.*

"And," Reggie continues, "we've got no sign of struggle or violence or foul play."

"Doesn't mean there wasn't any," I say. "But I agree. It looks like suicide. And it's possible the note is about the attempted break-in at her house and the poisonings, but it's so general that it might not be."

"I agree," she says, "but 'your grandma and her friends' makes me think he's referring to the poisonings."

"Certainly possible," I say. "He could've been trying to punish her grandmother and or the others or get them out of the way. No way to know what he was thinking."

"I know it's anticlimactic to have the murderer off himself," she says, "but . . . it's never a bad result. Still, you kill a little old lady and you deserve a lot worse than this."

58

"He's always struggled with . . . his . . . mental health," Donnie Ray's sister, Clarissa, is saying. "Never lived an easy day in his life. Some people don't. And it's . . . something others don't see. It's not like physical handicap or injury. Fact is . . . Donnie looked a little like a movie star. Never had any trouble getting girls. Always looked good outwardly. Nobody could tell how . . . injured he was."

"Had he mentioned taking his own life?" Reggie asks.

"Nearly his entire life," she says. "So . . . But no more lately than any other time. And he'd never really . . . tried anything before."

"Never?" I ask.

"Not that I'm aware of. Oh God. I still can't believe he's gone. Why didn't he call me? I could've . . . I would've done something."

"I'm very sorry," I say.

"And you didn't know he was here?" Reggie says. "He wasn't supposed to be?"

"No. Right. He . . . Since he split up with Lillian Pritchett . . . he hasn't really had a regular place to live. He crashed with us some—surfed a few couches at a few random friends' houses, but . . . I guess I didn't put it together until now, but he . . . he was homeless. Oh my God. I . . . I let my little brother be . . . homeless. How could I . . . I didn't mean to, but . . . that's what I did. And now he's . . . dead."

She breaks down and cries again, and we wait.

"I was surprised not to find a lot of meds," I say. "Was he on prescription medication or did he take other substances?"

She nods as she wipes at her eyes. "Yeah, both."

"We didn't find any meds or drugs or even empty bottles in the house or his car," Reggie says.

"Really?"

"That surprises you?" I say.

"Very much. He wasn't a neat person. His car was always trashed and it always had pill and alcohol bottles rattling around the floorboards. I'm really surprised you didn't find any. Maybe he had turned over a new leaf. Always said he was going to. If he was living in his car . . . Maybe he cleaned it. I don't know."

"How did he get his meds?" I ask.

"Disability," she says. "Government paid for them."

"And his drugs?"

"I don't want to think about what all he did to get those," she says. "I begged and pleaded with him, but . . . I'm pretty sure he did the usual . . . unsavory things . . . but I don't know for sure. And don't want to know. Especially now."

"Any idea who any of his suppliers were?" Reggie asks.

"Only one," she says. "He came to our house a few times and I had to pay him to get him to leave us alone. Not sure of his real name, but Donnie called him T-Rex."

59

Jasmine's funeral, like her mother's before, is a sad and pitiful affair.

The sky is gray, the planet beneath it monochrome, the atmosphere pregnant with rain that won't fall.

We stand in a large, flat, open, uncovered field around a coffin suspended on a lowering device over a freshly dug hole in the earth. The new cemetery, established a few years ago because the other one is full, has only a few headstones in a treeless field that not long ago was a cow pasture.

There are only a few of us present—and standing six feet apart from each other makes us seem even fewer than what we are.

At Nash's request, I am with him, and Paul is not allowed to be present.

The only others in attendance are Jules, Lavinia, Lillian, and Harley—who Lillian has yet to let go of for more than a few minutes at a time.

No church service. No hymns. No eulogy. No reading of the obituary. No memorial. Only a short graveside gathering.

The officiate, a female spiritualist from Sandcastle, may be doing a fine job, but I have no idea. I'm so focused on Nash that I hear very little of what she is saying.

Nash is broken, and I am broken for him.

He's awkward and lost, and seeing him in so much pain and discomfort causes a severe ache in my core that emanates outward into every part of my being, throbbing excruciatingly like an exposed nerve jangling with arches of raw pain.

I desperately want to do something for him that I am unable to—take away his pain, give him his mother back. But there are other things I can do for him, and I plan to do them—plan to do all I can for him.

His fragile, frightened question *What will happen to me?* echoes through my head and vibrates through my body.

What will happen to him? What will I do about it?

I know what I want to do, what I feel like I'm supposed to do, but I've got to talk to Anna, and I wonder what her reaction will be. After all we've been through, I hesitate to ask her for something so enormous, but I have to.

When the minister asks if anyone wants to say something, Nash steps forward.

"My mom was a good person," he says. "A good mom. She didn't have all her shit together, but . . . who does? She wasn't much of a housekeeper or cook. And . . . she . . . to be honest . . . she had bad taste in guys and some pretty weird ideas. But she had a good heart. She was a good person. She was good to me and my . . . my little brother. I will . . . miss her."

60

———

"**A**re you sure?" Anna asks.

"I am," I say.

We are on our back porch watching the girls play, backlit by the setting sun sinking behind the cypress trees rimming Lake Julia. The soft plum-colored glow reflects on the clear sky above and the surface of the lake below.

"Absolutely positive?" she asks.

"Yes," I say. "I am absolutely positive."

Nash is in his room having asked us if it was okay if he didn't join us like he usually does. The funeral had taken a lot of out him, and it was obvious he needed to be alone.

I just don't want him to be alone too long.

"I worry about us," she says. "With our recent issues related to my . . . condition, how demanding our jobs are, all the girls require, which is only increasing, what we do for Carla and John Paul, which is also increasing."

"I know," I say. "It's a lot. Too much in some ways. And adding to it is risky. It's a big ask, and I know it. I'm asking it fully aware of the commitment required and the implications, but I know we're up to it. Your health is so much better now. And we're good. If we stay centered and focused on us—"

"That's what I'm saying," she says. "That's hard to do as it is —with so much pulling on us, so much pulling us in different directions. I'm just scared."

"I know. And I wish I could tell you it's irrational, but it's not. I can only tell you that I believe we're supposed to do this and I also believe we'll be okay."

"I love you, John Jordan," she says. "And I love that you want to take in Nash. I do. And I'll do it for you. I'll do anything for you. You know that. I hope you know that. But I feel like there's somebody you want to adopt or help or save in nearly every case you work, and we can't—"

"Anna, Nash is our son from my recurring dream."

"What?" she says. "I thought it was John Paul and our daughters."

"It is," I say. "It's all of them. The dream is about all of them, but . . . it's about Nash too. I know it now. I couldn't before . . . because I hadn't met him yet, but it is. I know it's hard to . . . Trying to explain a dream is like trying to diagram a joke, or dance a poem, but . . . I believe it's about him."

"That's good enough for me," she says. "But it begs the question— What about his little brother?"

61

———

"A few days ago when you were saying that you didn't want to live with Paul," I say, "you said something to the effect that he wouldn't want you to anyway. Well, I want you to know that we want you. Anna and I would love to—"

"Even after what I painted on the Chinese restaurant?"

"Of course," I say.

Nash and I are in his room—him sitting on the bed, me on the floor a few feet away.

"I want to . . . Would it be okay if I . . . Could I live with you guys?"

"Absolutely," I say. "That's what I came up here to tell you. We would love that. We want you to."

"Really?"

"One hundred percent."

Though he seems no less sad than he has been for the past few days, he does seem relieved and less anxious.

"What has just happened to you is one of the worst things that can happen to someone," I say, "and you're in shock. And it will take a long time to process everything and to figure out what you really want. It's easy to make choices and decisions now that you may regret or want to change later."

"Okay?" he says, making the hesitant one-word question convey so much.

"So you can change your mind at any time," I say. "We will support you and help you throughout your entire life no matter what you decide to do or where you decide to live. But Anna and I have already talked about it and we'd love for you to join our family."

"Really?" he asks again.

"You don't have to decide anything now and if you do decide something now and want to change it later that's fine, but I want you to know that we think you're an amazing young man and we think the world of you. We'd be lucky to have you in our family if you decide you'd like to join us. But even if you don't, we will help you and support you and take care of you no matter what you do, where you go, or where you decide to live."

My words seem to have the impact I hoped they would.

He begins to cry, a flood of emotion pouring forth from him.

I join him.

"I . . . love . . . my mom," he says. "Nothing . . . against . . . her. And . . . But . . . to be honest . . . I was going to ask you if I could live here even before this happened."

MONDAY, MAY 18, 2020

Monday, May 18, 2020

1,498,266 confirmed cases and 84,231 deaths in the US

Though the number of coronavirus cases and deaths continue to rise, the majority of states move forward with phased-in reopenings that differ from county to county and city to city.

The CDC publishes a longer sixty-page document providing guidance to businesses, restaurants, schools, and other establishments on how to reopen while minimizing the risk of spreading the virus.

There are now over five million confirmed cases of the coronavirus worldwide—with the US accounting for nearly a third.

62

"He ain't goin' anywhere with you," Paul Branch is saying. "He's staying here in his home with me."

I'm not sure where he's been, but he arrives back home as Nash and I are loading the last of his things into my truck, and his breath smells of booze.

"I'm moving in with John and Anna," Nash says. "And don't you dare act like you give two shits about where I go or what happens to me."

Paul steps toward Nash and I step in between them.

"Oh, look who's a badass behind a badge and gun."

"It's okay," I say to Nash. "Go ahead and get in the truck."

"You only want him for the same reason I do," Paul says. "'Cause he gets him mama's money."

I glance at Nash who still hasn't moved and see that his face is a mask of pain and anger, his sad, red eyes tearing up again.

"I hope you know with absolute certainty that that's not true," I say to Nash. "I love you and believe God gave you to me to take care of—something I'll always do my best to do. I'll never ever touch a single cent of your money. I hope you'll put it up for college—but it's yours and you can do whatever you want to with it. I want you, not your money. Do you know that?"

He looks at me and nods.

"Think about all the time we've spent together," I say. "Had nothing to do with money."

He nods more vigorously.

"I'll always take care of you," I say. "Protect you from people like Paul. And I'll do that," I add, taking off my badge and taking out my gun and locking them in the truck, "not as a cop, but as . . . your dad if you'll have me. Paul is younger, faster, and stronger than me. Nobody wins in a fight, but I will likely lose a lot more than him and could get hurt pretty badly. I'd do that for you."

As ill-advised as this idiotic stunt is, I hope it conveys to Nash that he is loved and wanted, safe and secure, the opposite of an orphan. I'm desperate to demonstrate my love for and protection of him—to reassure him that even after all the loss and chaos and turmoil, he has someone in this world he can count on.

I look back at Paul. "I'm not a badass and I don't have a gun or a badge. All I want to do is what's best for Nash. I'm taking him with me. He's part of our family. Anna and I will take good care of him. We will spend our money on him and never touch any of his. Don't suppose you'll let us go without kicking my ass first?"

"Not on your life," he says.

I nod and circle away from Nash, widening my stance and bringing my arms up, bracing for Paul's attack.

I don't have to wait long.

He lunges toward me, and I turn to the side and shove him. He goes flying by.

He doesn't make that mistake again.

When he comes at me again, it's much slower and in a boxer's stance.

He throws a looping left I am able to block. Then a wild right with the same result.

I decide not to counter any of his punches, concentrating instead on blocking them, hoping he will punch himself out and give up.

Paul works out. Has plenty of muscle to show for it. But he's not a boxer and he doesn't have the kind of stamina it takes to sustain a fight. If I can just keep his punches from their intended targets and take the brunt of the vicious blows on my arms, I might be able to mitigate the damage he does.

All good in theory, but in actual practice he feints a left hook and as I go to block it, jumps at me and brings his right fist down in a hammer punch on my left temple that snaps my head down and to the side and makes me lose my equilibrium, causing my knees to buckle.

I go down hard, my head receiving a second blow from striking the ground.

For a moment, as I'm lying flat on my back, my head spinning like the rotating earth beneath me, time seems to stop. But only for a moment.

Suddenly, Paul is on top of me, pounding my head with his fists.

I try to raise my guard, but my arms aren't working.

And just as suddenly as his barrage of punches started, they stop.

Is my obvious defeat enough for him?

I had believed he wouldn't stop until I was unconscious or dead.

I look up, squinting through quickly swelling eyes to see Paul raising his hands above his head.

I rotate my head slightly and see that Nash is behind Paul, pointing my Glock at his head.

Feeling my now empty pocket, I realize that my keys must have fallen out at some point and Nash must have grabbed them in order to get in the truck and get my gun and maybe save my life.

He's far enough away so that Paul can't spin around and knock it out of his hand, and I wonder if it's on purpose.

"Nash," I say. "There's no safety on that weapon and the trigger is very sensitive. Be very, very careful. Take your finger off the trigger."

"Get off of him," Nash yells at Paul.

"Okay, okay," he says.

"Move off me to the opposite side of Nash," I say to Paul.

"Okay. Okay. Just don't shoot me, kid."

As Paul climbs off me, I try to get up, but my equilibrium is still off and every time I get on my feet, I lean and fall back over.

With the gun still pointed at Paul, Nash steps over to me and helps me up.

When I'm upright he hands me the gun, and I lean on him as we back our way to the truck.

"Go ahead and go," Paul says. "Good riddance. And I'll always be the man who kicked your ass."

"Don't get too excited," I say. "It's not that unique of a distinction."

63

____

As I crank the truck and try to get my bearings, I realize I know who killed Nell and Jasmine and why. It had come to me as I was lying flat on the earth and became clearer as I thought about being down there.

I also realize that I have to act immediately to prevent another death from occurring—the murder of a true innocent who had nonetheless caused a death. And it may already be too late.

I make a quick calculation regarding Nash.

Like all my parenting decisions, I make my best judgement without knowing for sure if it's the best choice I can make—though that is my intention.

"Thank you," I say as I pull away from the house. "You may have saved my life. You definitely kept me from a more severe concussion and potential brain damage."

"Knew you didn't need any more of that," he says with a smile.

I laugh. "No doubt."

He rarely makes comments like that so when he does they make me laugh even harder, appreciate him even more.

I turn out of his old neighborhood and toward Pottersville.

"Not sure I could've shot him," he says.

"Glad he didn't force you to find out."

"I wanted to," he says.

"That makes the fact that you didn't all the more noble. Shows great restraint. He said and did some horrible things to you. All of them are on him—what he is, what he is not. Has absolutely nothing to do with you. It shows great restraint that you didn't shoot him. I'm proud of you."

"I knew you wouldn't want me to."

"The people who do the most damage to us—or try to—are the most damaged. Or the most ignorant, immature, underdeveloped. The sooner we can see that what they say and do is about them far more than us, the better we can maintain our equilibrium and live the lives we want to—based on our code and conviction—and not in reaction to them."

"If I do get any money from Mom or Grandma," he says, "I want you to use some of it to help with expenses and—"

"I meant what I said. I will never touch a dime of it. It's the parents' job to take care of their kids. Not the other way around. I hope you'll put it up for college and a good start in life. And see it as your mother and grandmother still taking care of you."

Tears glisten in his eyes as he nods. "I do. I will."

"You've been through so much already," I say. "Far more than anyone should ever have to. But unfortunately, it's not quite over yet."

"It's not?"

"I think I know who killed your mother and grandmother and—"

"Who?"

"Lavinia," I say. "And I think your little brother's in danger. I can drop you off somewhere, but I thought you'd—"

"I want to go with you," he says.

"You sure?"

He nods.

"I wouldn't take you if I didn't know you were strong and mature enough to handle it," I say. "And I know if I were you, I'd want to be there to confront the person who killed my mom and grandma and try to save my little brother."

"I do."

"Okay," I say.

"Why would she kill them?" he says.

"It came to me as I was lying out flat on the earth," I say, "so in a way Paul helped me see it. You know how your grandmother and mother were into conspiracy theories and alternative—"

"Yeah," he says. "Shit like the earth is flat and the moon landing was faked."

"And that vaccinations cause autism," I say. "You and your brother have never been vaccinated—your mother either."

"It's why we gotta be homeschooled."

"Exactly. When your grandmother and Lavinia were arguing at Jules's birthday party, your grandmother said something about Lavinia living in fear and brokering in conspiracy theory nonsense—like 5G, the deep state, chem trails, and the coronavirus being a hoax, and Jules walked in and said something about Nell having her own share of crazy theories, like body earthing, essential oils, crystals, and anti-vaxing. I remember Lavinia started to say something else but stopped short. I think that's when she put it together that Lilliana got the whooping cough that killed her from Harley. She blamed your grandmother and mother for the death of her great-grandchild and the unbearable pain her precious Lilly was in."

"Did he?" he asks. "Did Harley give Lilliana—"

"I don't know," I say. "But I think Lavinia thinks that your mom or Harley gave it to Lillian who passed it on to Lilliana, causing her to kill her own child."

64

———————

"John," Jules says, "she was poisoned too. And she wasn't even at Nell's party. She's about the only one it couldn't be."

"She poisoned herself and you to cover what she was doing," I say. "Remember what she said—that when you ladies left the den on the way to the theater, she stopped into the bathroom in the hall while Nell used the one in the theater? Well, she couldn't've used that one—Dixie was in it at the time. Carla had to wait until Dixie came out to go to the theater and make sure everything was ready for the toast, but when she got there Lavinia, who was the first to arrive, was already in the dressing room—something she couldn't've been if she was still in line because Dixie just got out. She lied about using the hall bathroom and instead used that time to rush into your room to get the poison and take it to the theater to put it in the honey. She was one of the few who knew about the honey and had the opportunity to do it. I don't know if she meant to give Nell more to kill her at your party or if her goal was just to set up herself as a victim and confuse everyone, so she could kill her later without being suspected."

"But she didn't kill her. She wasn't even there."

"Sure she was," I say. "She was disguised as Charles Harbuck. I'm sure that's why Nell felt so confident. Lavinia told her it'd be their little secret until after the party was over—Nell even mentioned having a secret weapon or a surprise or a special announcement or something."

"She . . ."

"Think about it," I say. "It was her. Like you, she's a consummate performer. It was easy for her to transform herself into that character. And it wasn't the first time she had done it. She disguised herself as the guy trying to break into Lillian's home —to take any suspicion off Lillian and herself and to get Lillian to move in with her. And by having gloves and a mask on, she protected herself from the cyanide, which she dropped into Nell's glass while pretending to taste test the champagne as Charles Harbuck. Everyone thought Nell was trusting her favorite cousin, but it was her dear, close friend she was really placing her faith in. Makes the betrayal all the more bitter."

"But—"

"Have you ever met her favorite cousin before?" I ask.

"Well, no, but—"

"And y'all were best friends for how many decades?" I say. "And she helped you put everything back in the trunk as Charles—that's when she pocketed Nell's glass with the traces of cyanide in it."

"I'm not saying you're not making sense or it doesn't add up, but—"

"Remember when we went in search of Charles Harbuck and he was in the restroom? That's because she was talking to Lillian on the phone. And did you notice how she didn't show up to check on y'all until after Charles was gone? I'm sure she drove down the road a little ways and changed clothes and took the appliances and makeup off her face. There was so much going on, everyone distracted and in shock—no one noticed it was the same vehicle. You even commented on the fact that she didn't have any makeup on—but she didn't come soon enough after talking to Lillian to have rushed over and not had time to put makeup on. Now, tell me where she is."

"She took Harley to play at the park."

65

———

"**G**randma?" Lillian asks.

Her voice is that of an innocent little girl discovering her first deep dark secret about her primary caregiver. Shock. Sadness. Incomprehension. Disbelief. Disdain.

I had called for backup on the way, and not only had the two deputies arrived before us but they came in with lights flashing and had alerted Lavinia to what was going on.

By the time Nash and I and Jules and Lillian arrive, Lavinia has climbed up the small plastic roof covering the highest slide, which puts her and little Harley nearly thirty feet in the air.

She is holding Harley, who is crying, over the edge, sitting so close to edge of the sloping plastic herself that she could slide off at any moment.

Dad has arrived with additional deputies and cleared the area, so it's only me, Nash, Jules, and Lillian standing in the sand beneath the enormous steel and plastic commercial playground contraption. A growing group of gawkers have to watch from the perimeter.

"*Grandma,*" Lillian says again. "*Please.*"

"They killed your child," she says. "Made you think you did it. His evil mother and grandmother. They murdered our baby girl. Think about what they've put us through. So ignorant and radical and . . . I'm so sick of Nell and Jasmine and the deadly diseases they spread. They don't even care that they murdered our sweet little baby in cold blood. I couldn't let them live, couldn't bear to see them enjoying their lives like nothing had happened, like they hadn't taken everything from us."

"You okay?" I whisper to Nash.

He nods.

Lavinia has yet to look at him, and though he seems to want to, he hasn't said anything to her yet.

"I'm sorry you're seeing this," I say to him, "but I figured having you here would make it harder for her to hurt Harley. I feel like it's better if we just let Lillian talk."

"Grandma, *no*," Lillian says. "Even if I got it from them and gave it to Lilliana . . . it's not Harley's fault. He didn't get to choose what did or didn't happen to him any more than she did. Or I did. Please back up some and pull him back in. *Please*."

I had wondered if Lillian was involved in or knew anything about what her grandmother had done. Now I know. She couldn't be more shocked and horrified.

"They did it *to* him, to *you*, to *us*," Lavinia says. "From the moment I heard, I knew I couldn't let them . . . keep . . . living, knew I had to do something about it. I couldn't let them keep walkin' around in all their smelly superior left-wing hippie ignorance, living their lives like they hadn't destroyed us, destroyed *you*. They committed murder so nonchalantly and weren't even sorry. They knew what they were doing. Knew how many at-risk people, infants, children were involved. And they didn't care. There's no telling how many they've killed. They're responsible. It's murder. They murdered our precious little girl. They destroyed us."

"Grandma, I'm not destroyed. I'm still here."

"I wish I could've killed them with my bare hands," she says. "I really do. I would've loved to wrap my hands around their necks and choke the life out of them. Poison was too quick and easy and not painful enough. They deserved to be tortured, to suffer the way you have, the way sweet little Lilliana did."

"Nothing has done more for me since I lost my little Lilliana than taking care of that sweet, precious, innocent little boy. Don't take that from me."

"*What?*"

"I love that little fella," she says. "Please don't take him away from me. I can't watch another sweet, innocent child die. I can't. That would destroy me. And if you blame him for unwittingly giving me whooping cough, then you've got to blame me for unwittingly giving it to Lilliana. Are you going to kill me too?"

"*What?* No. Of course not."

Jules says, "Lavinia, you've seen how different Lillian's been since she's been keeping Harley. Don't take that away from her."

Lavinia seems confused and not quite sure what to do.

"These morons are endangering all of us," she says.

At first I'm not sure who she's talking about.

"They've never seen the pain and suffering and death of preventable diseases," she says. "They're so stupid. Vaccines working are the reason they have the luxury of their ignorance. Them and their silly celebrity puppets."

I think about all the conspiracy theories Lavinia believes and how much real damage they do to innocent people every day. Like her insistence that the coronavirus is a hoax. She's not denouncing conspiracy theories or objectively false claims or verifiably untrue assertions in general, just the ones she happens not to subscribe to.

"They murdered my precious, sweet little . . . great-grand-baby. My so-called friend and her daughter. I already lost a daughter. I couldn't do it, couldn't go through that again . . . But they didn't give me a choice. It is, you know—it's murder. They murdered our sweet little Lilliana just as surely as— I'm . . . My arms are getting tired." She looks back at Lillian. "If you want him you better come get him."

Lillian rushes up the stairs.

"Let me help you down too," she says.

"I'm not coming down," Lavinia says. "Least not alive. This was a one-way trip for me—thought for both of us, but . . . definitely for me."

"Grandma," Lillian says. "Please don't. I need—"

"Take him, quick," she says.

After handing Harley down to Lillian, who holds and hugs him like her own, Lavinia reaches into her pocket and brings out a small vial. Quickly removing the lid, she leans her head back and ingests its contents.

"*Grandma, NO*," Lillian yells.

I turn to Nash. "Turn around," I say. "Don't look."

"She killed my mama," he says. "I'm not looking away."

"I'm not sorry," Lavinia says. "I'd do it all again. Nothing's more important than family. Protecting it is our—"

She begins gasping for breath as she clutches at her heart.

Falling back, she beings to writhe and convulse. But not for long.

As her body stops seizing, she begins to slide off the edge, and as it pitches forward, I turn and pull Nash into me, blocking his view of her fall to the ground.

He doesn't resist my efforts to shield him, and is spared from seeing the horror on display.

What I am unable to shield him from, however, is the savage sound her body makes as it strikes the unforgiving surface of the earth.

66

———

"How do you become that?" Jules is saying. "I don't recognize that—*her*. How could you do that to one of your best friends and her daughter and nearly to a toddler?"

"Obsession," I say. "Compulsion. Vengeance. Retribution. Unchecked anger. All fueled by grief—and not just hers but by that of her only granddaughter too. And Max has had her in an echo chamber of hate and paranoia and conspiracy theories for the past several years. It's unimaginably extreme and shows signs of real mental illness, but . . . nearly everyone can understand the desire to destroy those who you believe murdered your innocent little great-grandchild and irrevocably broke your granddaughter's very being. "

Dad and I have just stopped by Jules's and find Merrill and Zaire with her. Lillian, still holding Harley and giving no indication that she will ever let him go again, is on the back porch in a rocking chair, gazing out at the river.

After I made sure Nash was okay, Anna picked him up and took him home while I stayed to help work the crime scene.

"I just can't . . ." Jules says. "I know I'm still in shock, but . . . I'm not sure I'll ever be able to truly believe it's real. No matter how long I live. I've just realized that no matter how long that is —it will be without my two best friends. That can't . . . Somebody wake me up and tell me that can't really be the case."

"I wish I could," Dad says. "I'm so sorry for all you've lost."

"How did she kill poor Jasmine?" Jules asks.

"Don't know for certain," I say, "but I believe she poisoned some of the meds she was on—emptied out a couple of capsules and replaced their contents with poison. It would've been easy enough for her to do during a quick visit—or even at Nell's birthday if Jasmine had the pills in her purse or car. We know she knew Jasmine was taking medication—she mentioned it when Nell died. She would have no way of knowing exactly when Jasmine would take them, but whenever it was, she wouldn't be anywhere around her."

We all grow quiet for a long moment.

Eventually Jules says, "Are there really people who don't vaccinate their children?"

"A growing number of them," Zaire says. "And just like with the coronavirus, their actions have a huge impact on others. It's all part of the wacky world of paranoid nutters who reject science and mistrust government and are attracted to the most insane conspiracy theories. Some are religious flat-earthers. Some are anti-establishment celebrity sycophants. None of them have ever seen the ravages of what preventable diseases can do. Mark my words. Even when we develop a vaccine for COVID-19, a large percentage of people won't take it."

"How can that even be?" Jules says. "What the hell happened to my world?"

"People are living in idiosyncratic echo chambers that feed their basest biases," I say, "a swirl of culture, religion, politics, race, and worldview that confirms for us that we're right to hold the opinions we do—no matter how outlandish or verifiably wrong they may be—and everyone else is wrong."

"I just don't get any of this," she says. "Our world is so sick. In so many ways."

"We definitely have more than one pandemic happening right now," I say. "The internet and social media play a big part, but this started way before they were created. So-called reality TV, partisan propaganda parading as news. Opinion and theories replacing facts. And acting as if everybody's opinion is equal—even to educated experts. It's a virus and it's spread into the mainstream of our cultural bloodstream. It's not fringe anymore."

Zaire says, "Religious leaders, gurus, politicians, opinion makers, internet influencers, and crazy old Uncle Joe up in the attic all have a voice, a platform, a forum with zero accountability and that goes unchecked."

"Leave Uncle Joe out of this," Merrill says.

"Most people are sheep," she says. "They have a herd mentality. They're tribal. Irrational—especially when fearful. Self-centered. And highly manipulatable."

"I knew Nellie Bell and Lavinia believed some crazy, window-licker kind of stuff," Jules says. "I mean, their shtick was arguing about it—but I never dreamed it was this dangerous. I still can't believe I didn't see it, didn't realize it was her. Of course, I don't know why. Even now I can't bring myself to really believe it was."

"The thing is, we all have biases," I say, "and are constantly searching for confirmation for them—without even realizing it. We're all sitting here with them right now—not even aware of most of them. We've got to make a concerted effort to fight against just going with them."

Merrill says, "Good start is listening to vetted experts and scientist and journalists."

"But," Zaire says, "the unvetted more often say what we want to hear. Lot easier just to yell *fake news* at the truth we don't like to hear."

"What kind of world is my generation leaving behind for y'all?" Jules says.

MONDAY, MAY 25, 2020

Monday, May 25, 2020

1,649,054 confirmed cases and 91,971 deaths in the US

At least 1 confirmed case of murder of a cuffed, unarmed
black man.

Memorial Day weekend brings Americans outside, many of
whom do not practice social distancing. Photos emerge of busy
beaches and bustling pool parties.

WHO says it is temporarily dropping hydroxychloroquine
from its study of experimental COVID-19 treatments.

More than one hundred thousand people have died in the
US after contracting the coronavirus since the first fatality,
believed to have occurred back on February 6, 2020, in
California.

GEORGE FLOYD

On what would've been Lavinia's seventy-fourth birthday, George Perry Floyd Jr., a forty-six-year-old African American Minnesota man is murdered by a police officer who keeps his knee on Floyd's neck for over eight minutes after he is cuffed and lying facedown on the ground.

The horrific incident is captured on a cell phone video camera by a bystander.

Floyd is shown pleading with the police officer for his life, repeatedly telling him he can't breathe.

Shortly before he breathes his last breath, Floyd calls for his mother, who had passed away years ago.

The viral video of this sadly all-too-common event sparks worldwide protests against racism and police brutality against black people.

Floyd's death followed the February 23 murder of Ahmaud Arbery, a twenty-five-year-old unarmed black man, who was hunted down and killed in cold blood while out jogging by three white men near Brunswick, Georgia, and the March 13 death of Breonna Taylor, a twenty-six-year-old Louisville ER technician, shot eight times in her own home when police entered in the early morning hours on a no-knock narcotics warrant.

The resulting global protests and Black Lives Matter programs have been extraordinary and transformative. Continuing at an unprecedented rate, they include people of all races. In fact, in some cities, African American protesters have been in the minority.

67

A few days later, both disturbed and inspired by what is happening in the country, Merrill walks into Dad's office.

I follow closely behind him, grateful to get to witness what is about to transpire.

"If the job offer's still good, I'd like to accept it," Merrill says.

Dad stands and comes around his desk and extends his hand, but when Merrill gets close enough, he breaks all protocol and wraps his arms around him and gives him a hug.

"Thank you, son," he says. "You don't know what this means to me—and how good it'll be for the department. It looks as if our country and our law enforcement agencies are rife for reform. Let's make our little rural South department a leader."

"Not sure the department is ready for that . . ." he says. "But I damn sure am."

"We'll get them ready," Dad says. "If it was easy, anybody could do it."

.   .   .

As Merrill and I are walking out, we encounter a thirty-something white deputy who walks and talks like a young John Wayne.

"Rumor goin' around you might be joining our department," he says.

Merrill nods warily. "You the welcomin' committee?"

"I just try to be helpful to everyone I can," he says, "but don't expect too many of the men to be real welcoming. This affirmative action or whatever they call it these days . . . Some see it as putting you in a position some good cops already here deserved. And hey, I get with how things are right now the sheriff is tryin' to . . . But you should know straight up that around here we believe all lives matter."

"Wasn't affirmative action or quotas, but hard work, experience, intelligence, and a thousand other qualities that earned Merrill this job."

"Bein' best friends with the sheriff's son don't hurt none, I bet."

"Got nothing to do with it," I say.

"I ain't sayin' that's how I see it," he says. "I just figured you'd want to know how some of the others see it."

"And to say all lives matter in the context of the Black Lives Matter movement when unarmed black men are being murdered in the streets and the vast majority of black people in this country are subjected to inequality and systemic racism and oppression every single day is far, far worse than just ignorantly stating the obvious. It's like being attacked and going to the hospital injured and bleeding and having the ER just telling you that everybody's health is important. It's like having a house burning down in your neighborhood and you and your other neighbors blocking the street to tell the firefighters that your house is just as important as the house that's on fire. It'd be like hearing Jesus say, 'Blessed are the poor,' and you saying, 'No, Jesus. Blessed is everybody.'"

"I get it. I get it. I'm just trying to help. I'm tellin' you as a friend. It's a crazy time right now. Got this virus spreading like wildfire and protestors looting the—"

"Protestors aren't looting," Merrill says. "They're protesting —99.9 percent of them, peacefully. Looters are looting. They are not protesting. Never were."

"Y'all are takin' everything I'm sayin' the wrong way," he says. "All I'm tryin' to do is say *welcome aboard* and let you know how things are around here."

"Actually," Merrill says, "that's how things *were* around here. But not anymore. It's been a long time coming, but a change is gonna come." And then he adds in his best MLK voice, "How long?"

"Not long," I say on cue.

"How long?" he says again.

"Not long."

He then begins to recite the Black National Anthem in the same voice, quoting it like the poem it originally was instead of singing it like we had done so many times together at the Black History Month programs in the chapel of Potter Correctional Institution.

"Lift every voice and sing," he says.

"'Til earth and heaven ring," I say, continuing the refrain.

The deputy nods and gives us an awkward smile, then hurries away.

"Ring with the harmonies of liberty," Merrill says, as we continue out of the building and toward my truck. "Let our rejoicing rise."

"High as the listening skies," I say. "Let it resound loud as the rolling sea."

68

———

"We'd like to talk to you about something," I say to Nash.

It's been over a week since Lavinia killed herself.

We are all seated in our living room—Anna, Nash, me, and Lillian. Jules is down by the lake in the backyard with Johanna, Taylor, and Harley.

"Is it okay with you that I'm here?" Lillian asks Nash.

He nods.

I had already asked him before telling her it was okay for her to come over.

I look over at Nash. "We want to talk to you about Harley," I say. "Want you to get to make the decision about what happens to him."

"Okay."

"As his biological father," I say, "Paul has custody rights, but he hasn't really exercised them. He's let Lillian keep him . . . well, really this entire time."

Nash shakes his head in disgust. "Better for him anyway."

"We think so too," Anna says.

"There are only a few options," I say, "and we want you to get to decide between them. The first is leave him with Paul and let Paul raise him."

"I vote against that one," he says.

"The second one is . . ." I say. "He won't let me or Anna keep him. He still holds a grudge against me, but he has indicated he would be willing to let Lillian adopt him."

"I want you to know how much I love him," Lillian says. "I . . . if I'm honest . . . I already feel like his mother. And I would do anything for him. I'd give him the best life I possibly can. I'd be so good to him. And I'd let you two spend as much time together as you want. But I understand if you don't want me to. I'm so very sorry for what my grandmother did to your mother and grandmother, and I would—"

"I'm sorry for what they did to your baby," he says.

Lillian bursts into tears and begins sobbing. "That's . . . so kind of you to say. Shows what a remarkable young man you are. The thing is . . . I feel like we could . . . well, we could all be a family of sorts. We're all connected through our grandmothers and aunts and I just feel . . . Anyway, I want to . . . More than anything in this world I want to be the best mother possible to your little brother, but I would understand if you wouldn't be comfortable with that."

"You should know," I say to Nash, "that Paul is only willing to do it if he gets the money from your grandmother's life insurance."

"Give it to him," he says. "I want Lillian to be Harley's mother. I don't care about the money."

A fresh wave of joyful sobs overtakes Lillian. "Are you sure?"

"Positive."

"There's another part to this," I say.

Lillian says, "We would only let Paul *think* he was getting your grandmother's life insurance money, but you and Harley would still get that. I would pay him and tell him it was Nell's life insurance money. Because that seems to be a real—"

Nash jumps up and rushes over to Lillian and sort of falls into her and hugs her and joins her in cathartic sobs.

When I glance over at Anna through tears of my own, I see she is also crying.

And on this day, during a global pandemic and a nation in protest over egregious racial injustice, a new extended family is formed in a sacred covenant cut with the shedding of tears.

69

"This can't be my first case," Merrill says.

"It's not."

"As a Potter County sheriff's investigator it would be."

It's the middle of the night. We are standing in the middle of Main Street just outside the pool of bright light the portable bank of LED lamps are illuminating the shocking crime scene with.

Main has been blocked off about a quarter of a mile in each direction, the flashing blue lights flickering at the edges where the circumference of the crime scene falls off into darkness.

What little overnight traffic there may be is being diverted down side streets and around this section of Main that is made up mostly of mainline Protestant churches.

"I'm not—I don't think I can do this."

"I don't think anyone but you can do it," I say. "I think you've been preparing your entire life for this."

From an enormous limb spreading out over Main Street on one of Pottersville's oldest and largest live oak trees, the body of a black man hangs from a noose.

It's a shocking and disturbing image fraught with the weight of an American holocaust, a reminder of our hateful history of legal tyranny and the too-often state-sanctioned terrorism on our own citizens.

Beneath the cover of the bottom-lit live oak, FDLE crime scene techs in bunny suits process the scene, as investigators from the ME's office await the cutting down of the body.

Merrill shakes his head. "I don't know . . . I just don't think I can. It's too raw. Too real. Too much a reminder."

Several years ago, when I was still a chaplain at Potter CI, I helped Dad investigate a case that involved a lynching out in the river swamp. It had been too much for Merrill then, and I understood, just as I do now—though I do believe what I said to him. He's the perfect person to investigate this.

"You think this is connected to California?" he asks.

"Hard to see how it's not."

In the past few weeks, two black men in California had been found hanging from trees. Malcolm Harsch, 38, was found on May 31 in Victorville, California, and then on June 10, Robert Fuller, 24, was found about fifty miles west in Palmdale.

Investigators said there were no indications at the scenes that suggested foul play. And though they also said that the cause and manner of death are pending, they gave every indication that the presumption was suicide in both cases. But public outcry has led to investigators taking a closer look at the cases.

"If Harsch and Fuller were suicides and our is too," I continue, "they could've inspired him in some way. If Harsch and Fuller were homicides and ours is too, then the murderer or murderers could've inspired our murderer or murderers. And vice versa. Murders could've inspired a suicide or suicides could've inspired a murder."

"No matter which it is," he says, "got to be related to George Floyd, the protests, the raised awareness of racism, the stirring of the melting pot, the civil unrest."

I nod. "And the impact of the pandemic and the quarantine. Everything's connected."

He frowns and shakes his head as he looks back at the man hanging from the tree. "Can you believe this shit ain't a hate crime?"

Recently, Kentucky Senator Rand Paul, a Republican, blocked the passage of legislation that would have made lynching a federal hate crime.

"I wish we lived in a world where I'd find that hard to believe."

Seeing the surreal hanging tree lit up against the night sky reminds me of the tree in front of the Jackson County courthouse in Marianna where Claude Neal was hung. I encountered it while working an unsolved case there with Dad involving Ted Bundy. That tree is said to be the spot of the last public lynching in America back in 1934, but Neal was already dead when the committee of six hung him from it.

Neal had been murdered the night before after being arrested for allegedly raping and murdering Lola Cannady, a nineteen-year-old white woman.

In the wake of the murder of George Floyd and others by police and the protest and civil unrest that has followed, a group called the Street Philosophy Institute created a petition calling for the removal of what has come to be known as the Claude Neal tree.

Though the petition has over 6,000 signatures, the NAACP chapter of Jackson County and the descendants of Claude Neal are in favor of the tree being preserved and not cut down.

I look at Merrill again, our eyes locking, connecting in a way only friends as old and as close as us can.

"It's your call, of course," I say. "I'm sure Dad would understand if you don't want to work it, and can assign it to someone else. But if you decide you do, I'll be with you every step of the way.

PLEASE POST A REVIEW

Please take a moment and post a review of this and other books by Michael Lister. It really helps and is greatly appreciated.

GET THE LATEST NEWS

Sign up for Michael's Readers' Group at www.MichaelLister.com and receive the latest news and reviews of the best in mystery, thriller, and crime fiction.

ALSO BY MICHAEL LISTER

Books by Michael Lister

(John Jordan Novels)

Power in the Blood

Blood of the Lamb

Flesh and Blood

(Special Introduction by Margaret Coel)

The Body and the Blood

Double Exposure

Blood Sacrifice

Rivers to Blood

Burnt Offerings

Innocent Blood

(Special Introduction by Michael Connelly)

Separation Anxiety

Blood Money

Blood Moon

Thunder Beach

Blood Cries

A Certain Retribution

Blood Oath

Blood Work

Cold Blood

Blood Betrayal

Blood Shot

Blood Ties

Blood Stone

Blood Trail

Bloodshed

Blue Blood

And the Sea Became Blood

The Blood-Dimmed Tide

Blood and Sand

A John Jordan Christmas

Blood Lure

Blood Pathogen

(Jimmy Riley Novels)

<u>The Girl Who Said Goodbye</u>

<u>The Girl in the Grave</u>

<u>The Girl at the End of the Long Dark Night</u>

<u>The Girl Who Cried Blood Tears</u>

<u>The Girl Who Blew Up the World</u>

(Merrick McKnight / Reggie Summers Novels)

<u>Thunder Beach</u>

<u>A Certain Retribution</u>

<u>Blood Oath</u>

<u>Blood Shot</u>

(Remington James Novels)

<u>Double Exposure</u>

<u>(includes intro by Michael Connelly)</u>

Separation Anxiety

Blood Shot

(Sam Michaels / Daniel Davis Novels)

<u>Burnt Offerings</u>

<u>Blood Oath</u>

<u>Cold Blood</u>

<u>Blood Shot</u>

(Love Stories)

<u>Carrie's Gift</u>

(Short Story Collections)

North Florida Noir

Florida Heat Wave

Delta Blues

Another Quiet Night in Desperation

(The Meaning Series)

<u>Meaning Every Moment</u>

<u>The Meaning of Life in Movies</u>